INVOLVED IN THE HIJINKS
IN SAN FRANCISCO WERE:

BARBARA ANN MILLER (a.k.a. BETSY BOOBS)—a curvaceous student nurse and honors graduate of Sadie Shapiro's Strip Joint, she was a dedicated angel of mercy, ever ready to serve her fellow man.

PANCHO HERMANEZ—A gifted balalaika player in a Parisian nightclub, he had spent his boyhood in a Russian Orthodox monastery, of all places!

FRANCIS BURNS, M.D.—a prosperous practitioner in the expanding field of vasectomology, the former Major Burns, Medical Corps, Korea, had earned undying fame with the broadcast of his timeless praise of Major Houlihan's burning lips.

COLONEL C. EDWARD WHILEY—A pillar of San Francisco society, he was to become the first man to pilot a plane *under* the Golden Gate Bridge.

Books in the MASH Series

Published by POCKET BOOKS

M★A★S★H
Goes to San Francisco

M*A*S*H
Goes to San Francisco

**Richard Hooker
and
William E. Butterworth**

PUBLISHED BY POCKET BOOKS NEW YORK

M*A*S*H GOES TO SAN FRANCISCO

POCKET BOOK edition published November, 1976

This original POCKET BOOK edition is printed from brand-new
plates made from newly set, clear, easy-to-read type.
POCKET BOOK editions are published by
POCKET BOOKS,
a division of Simon & Schuster, Inc.,
A GULF+WESTERN COMPANY
630 Fifth Avenue,
New York, N.Y. 10020.
Trademarks registered in the United States
and other countries.

ISBN: 0-671-80786-2.

Printed in the U.S.A.

In fond memory of
Malcolm Reiss,
gentleman literary agent

June 3, 1905–December 17, 1975
—Richard Hooker
and W. E. Butterworth

Chapter One

When Mrs. C. Edward Sattyn-Whiley, a rather formidable lady of generous proportions, rolled up to the main entrance of the San Francisco Opera House in her white Rolls-Royce, she was the cynosure of all eyes, which was, frankly, the way she both planned and wanted it.

Mrs. Sattyn-Whiley was the undisputed *grande dame* of San Francisco society, and she had dressed the part tonight. Her blue hair was topped with a diamond tiara, and she was actually wearing a stomacher, which is a piece of jewelry that hangs about the neck and terminates in a large jewel in the vicinity of the bellybutton.

She descended from the white Rolls-Royce, a 1935 model, the "Silver Ghost,"* rather regally on the arm of her husband of some thirty years, Colonel C. Edward Whiley, and was followed a moment later by her son, Cornelius E. Sattyn-Whiley, M.D.

Neither Colonel Whiley, a pale-faced chap who would have registered about 125 pounds on the scales if he and his top hat and tails were all soaking wet, nor his son, who took after his mother's side of the

* One of the reasons Mrs. Sattyn-Whiley was the *grande dame* of San Francisco society was her wealth. And one of the reasons she was wealthy was that she had four cents out of every nickel she had ever made and/or inherited. She had inherited the 1935 Rolls-Royce from her Uncle Max, and was not, as she told one Rolls-Royce salesman after another, going to buy a newer model so long as this one could be coaxed into life.

family and would have registered about 230 pounds on the scales, bone-dry, looked positively overjoyed at the prospect of an evening at the opera.

Dr. Cornelius E. Sattyn-Whiley had just returned to San Francisco after an extended absence, and tonight was, in a manner of speaking, his reintroduction to society. Cornelius Dear, as his mother called him, had, in fact, just returned from the jungles of the Northeast, where he had been educated, had graduated as a doctor of medicine, and had spent a year as an intern and then three years as a surgical resident—all at a large medical establishment that shall herein be unnamed, but which is located on the banks of the Charles River in a large city in Massachusetts.

Cornelius Dear was an only child, which had prompted his godfather, Dr. Aloysius J. Grogarty, to suggest that marital relations were something else that Mrs. C. Edward Sattyn-Whiley had tried once, found undignified, and never tried again.*

With her son and husband at her side, Mrs. Sattyn-Whiley marched into the grand foyer, acknowledged with a barely perceptible nod of her blue-haired head those few people whom she felt worthy of that honor, and then proceeded backstage. She felt that her position was such that it behooved her to visit the performers before a performance, to let them know, so to speak, that even if she *was* in the audience, they should not be nervous.

Most of the time, she was a bit uncomfortable with the singers, because the vast majority of them were not of her social class. Tonight, however, that wasn't the case. Tonight she would visit Madame Kristina Korsky-Rimsakov, who was singing the lead role in Giacomo Puccini's *Madame Butterfly*.

When Madame Korsky-Rimsakov had been first proposed, some six years before, as *the* prima donna of the San Francisco Opera—on the board of directors

---

* Dr. Grogarty had made this comment at Cornelius Dear's second birthday party. Mrs. Sattyn-Whiley had had the upstairs butler show him the door, and he had been *persona non grata* ever since.

of which Colonel C. Edward Whiley sat—Mrs. Sattyn-Whiley* had been aghast.

"Fifty thousand dollars a year!" she had commented. "That's an awful lot of money for a singer, Edward."

"Not for a singer like this one," her husband had (for once) argued. "She's been getting that much from the Metropolitan."

"So what?" Mrs. Sattyn-Whiley had responded. "What else do you know about her?"

"Her brother is the star of the Paris Opera," the colonel had replied.

"I don't like the French and never have," she'd said. "All they think about is sex."

"I don't think he's French," the colonel had replied. "Not with a name like that. Sounds more like Russian."

"Perhaps," Mrs. C. Edward Sattyn-Whiley had said, suddenly struck with an entirely pleasant notion, "they are both exiled Russian nobility!"

"I don't mean to sound argumentative, darling," the colonel had then said, quite unnecessarily, "but I hardly think that's possible. She's only in her late thirties, and the Russian Revolution was over fifty years ago."

"The children of impoverished noblemen!" Mrs. Sattyn-Whiley had cried. With that she'd picked up the telephone and called the San Francisco Public Library's Genealogical Collection. Within a matter of minutes, she'd been informed of the existence of the Grand Duke Sergei Korsky-Rimsakov, Lieutenant General of the Imperial Army, who was known to have fled to the West with his family in 1917.

"You see, Edward?" Mrs. Sattyn-Whiley had said. "I have a feeling about things like this. How soon did

---

* Perceptive readers may be wondering why it is Colonel Whiley and Mrs. Sattyn-Whiley. This is because Mrs. Sattyn-Whiley had announced, after the colonel had proposed to her, that she had no intention of permitting the Sattyn name, which went back all the way to the days of the Gold Rush of 1849 (Ezekiel Sattyn had owned 160 acres adjacent to Mr. Sutter), to die simply because her father's chromosomes had been the wrong kind to produce a son.

you say the grand duchess can join us here in San Francisco?"

If Mrs. C. Edward Sattyn-Whiley had been the sort of woman who could admit to having made a slight error of judgement, which she was not, she might have confessed to being somewhat disappointed in Madame Korsky-Rimsakov, at least personally. Not only did she *not* look like what Mrs. C. Edward Sattyn-Whiley thought a grand duchess should look like—she looked, actually, like the jolly and well-stuffed workers and peasants one sees in advertisements for travel in Russia—she also flatly refused to even discuss her family tree, other than to inform Mrs. Sattyn-Whiley that, so far as she knew, her only living relative was her brother Boris in Paris.

Worse, several years before, showing a shameful disregard for what Mrs. Sattyn-Whiley thought of as *noblesse oblige,* Madame Korsky-Rimsakov had married far beneath her. She had married, in fact, a man named J. Robespierre O'Reilly, who was nothing more than a short-order cook who'd made it big. Mr. O'Reilly's considerable fortune came from his chain of fast-food restaurants, which were known as Mother O'Reilly's Irish Stew Parlors.*

About the only kind thing Mrs. C. Edward Sattyn-Whiley could find to say about Mr. J. Robespierre O'Reilly was that he did have enough common decency, as she thought of it, to secretly donate to the Opera Guild an amount of money equal to that which the opera paid his wife.

Mr. O'Reilly was in Madame Kristina Korsky-Rimsakov's dressing room when Mrs. C. Edward Sattyn-Whiley, trailed by her husband and son, swept in.

"Good evening, Mr. O'Reilly," Mrs. Sattyn-Whiley said. "Do you suppose that the grand duchess might

---

* Those readers with a burning curiosity to know how a former corporal of the Medical Service Corps rose from dishwashing to command an empire of 2,108 stew parlors, worldwide, and to win the hand of Madame Korsky-Rimsakov, will find all the sordid details related in *M*A*S*H Goes to Las Vegas* (Pocket Books, New York).

possibly be gracious enough to grant me a moment of her time?"

"Who?" Mr. O'Reilly replied. "Oh, you mean *Kris!*" He turned his head slightly and called out, "Hey, pumpkin, you decent?" He turned to Colonel Whiley. "Hiya, Colonel," he said.

"Hello, Mr. O'Reilly," the colonel replied. His wife glowered at him.

Kristina Korsky-Rimsakov, already dressed for her role as Cio Cio San, came into the room.

"This your boy, Colonel?" Mr. O'Reilly asked. "Looks a lot like his mother. Well-stuffed, if you know what I mean."

"Robespierre!" Madame Korsky-Rimsakov said.

"Gee, pumpkin," Mr. O'Reilly said, getting his first look at her. "You look great! If I didn't know better, I'd say you were really one of those geisha girls."

"Thank you, dear," Madame Korsky-Rimsakov said.

"Gee, I just thought of something," Mr. O'Reilly said. "This opera you're going to sing isn't a dirty opera, is it?"

"Of course not, dear," Madame Korsky-Rimsakov said.

"Whatever possessed you to ask such a thing?" Mrs. Sattyn-Whiley demanded to know, her intention to ignore Mr. O'Reilly overcome by his violation of all that she held sacred.

"You wouldn't believe the things I could tell you about geisha girls," Mr. O'Reilly said. "And I bet you could, too, huh, Colonel? You went on R&R to Japan, too, didn't you? Boy!"

"I am sure, Mr. O'Reilly," Mrs. Sattyn-Whiley said, "that the colonel did not patronize establishments of the kind with which you are familiar."

"Oh, I know that," Mr. O'Reilly said. "I'm sure the colonel knows even more about it than I do. They kept the good ones just for the officers. But I heard the officers talk about it. That's about all they ever talked about. Would you believe that they take off everything but their underwear and then walk around on your back?"

13

"Robespierre, shut up!" Madame Korsky-Rimsakov said.

"Sorry, pumpkin," he said. "If you tell me this opera's not dirty, that's good enough for me."

"I just wanted to take a moment of your time, Your Highness," Mrs. Sattyn-Whiley said, "to tell you that we're all looking forward to your performance tonight."

"You know," Mr. O'Reilly said, "I checked the box office just before I came in here. It's sold out. I'll bet a lot of people out there think they're going to see something dirty."

The door to the dressing room was suddenly flung open. A bearded gentleman in full Arabian robes stepped in, and then, as he bowed low, announced in a loud voice, "His Royal Highness, the Sheikh of Abzug!"

Mrs. Sattyn-Whiley's mouth opened wide. A very large Arabian gentleman with a pointed beard swept into the room.

"Hey, Abdullah!" Mr. O'Reilly said. "You're early."

His Royal Highness, smiling broadly, bowed to Madame Kristina Korsky-Rimsakov. "Mud in your eye!" he said. He turned to Mrs. Sattyn-Whiley and bowed again. "Up yours!" he said. "Your mother wear army shoes!"*

"What did he say?" Mrs. Sattyn-Whiley inquired, aghast.

"His Royal Highness doesn't speak very much English," Madame Korsky-Rimsakov said, somewhat lamely. "I hope you misunderstood him."

"I bring greetings, my lady," the Sheikh said, switching to French, which Mrs. Sattyn-Whiley understood. "From your brother. I have just seen him and the baroness** in Paris."

---

* What few phrases of English His Royal Highness knew he had learned in the company of Mr. Boris Alexandrovich Korsky-Rimsakov in Paris. The details have been recorded for students of Arabian-American socio-economic affairs in *M*A*S*H Goes to Morocco* (Pocket Books, New York).

** His Highness here referred to the Baroness d'Iberville, one of Mr. Korsky-Rimsakov's very good friends.

"Did you?" Kristina Korsky-Rimsakov said.

"Hey, Abdullah," Mr. O'Reilly said. "Ix-nay! Ut-shay Uphay!" *

"My brother sometimes doesn't choose his friends with care," Madame Kristina, whose concept of sexual morality was somewhat at variance with that of the baroness, explained.

"I understand perfectly, Your Highness," Mrs. Sattyn-Whiley said. "The Baroness is beneath your brother."

"Is she ever!" Mr. O'Reilly replied. "Every time you turn your back."

Before the conversation could deteriorate further, decorum was restored by the bell announcing that the curtain would ascend in three minutes.

"I'm afraid you'll have to excuse me, Mrs. Sattyn-Whiley," Kristina said.

"I understand perfectly, Your Highness," Mrs. Sattyn-Whiley said. "Thank you for receiving us."

She made a double curtsy, first to Sheikh Abdullah and then to Madame Korsky-Rimsakov, and then made her exit, pulling her husband and her son after her.

"And she denies being a grand duchess!" she said, as she walked rapidly toward the Sattyn-Whiley box. "Well, I'll tell you this, I saw His Royal Highness' picture in the paper today. He's in San Francisco, it said, to visit old friends. And now we know who the old friend is, don't we? *The grand duchess,* that's who!"

"I got the impression, Mother Dear," Cornelius Dear said, "that he had come to see Mr. O'Reilly."

"Don't be absurd, Cornelius Dear," his mother said. "Whatever would someone of noble blood see in that horrid man?"

They got to their box just as the conductor entered the orchestra pit and the caterwauling of the instruments being tuned died with an agonized whimper.

---

* For those whose pig Latin is a little rusty, this, freely translated, is, "Stop it, shut up!"

Mounted directly above the proscenium arch in the San Francisco Opera is a small electrical device that, when activated, flashes a number on and off. Each practitioner of the medical arts is assigned a number, so that in case of medical emergency he can be summoned from his seat without the necessity of broadcasting his name over the public-address system, thereby disturbing the music lovers.

As the conductor rapped his baton on his music stand and then raised it preparatory to beginning the overture, the electrical device came to life. Number thirteen flashed on, then off, and then on again.

"Cornelius Dear," Mrs. Sattyn-Whiley said, "Mommy has another little surprise for you. Whenever that thing flashes number one, that will be for you."

"Number one? But Mother Dear, there are *hundreds* of physicians registered."

"That's true, Cornelius Dear," his mother said. "But their mommies aren't the chairperson of the Opera Guild, and their daddies don't sit on the board of directors."

The music began as the house lights went down. Number thirteen stopped flashing, indicating that healer number thirteen had seen it, and, true-blue to the Hippocratic oath, had left his seat to bring aid and comfort to his fellow man.

There was some Japanese-sounding music, and then the curtain rose. A Japanese gentleman and an officer of the United States Navy were at stage left.

Number one started to flash on and off on the device over the proscenium arch.

"Cornie," Colonel Whiley said, "they're flashing your number."

"I wish you wouldn't call him that," Mrs. Sattyn-Whiley hissed. "It's undignified for a doctor of medicine, not to mention someone named Sattyn-Whiley."

"I'll have to go," Dr. Sattyn-Whiley said.

"If I'd known they would call you from the opera," Mother Dear said, "I would have gotten you an unlisted number."

Dr. Cornelius Sattyn-Whiley made his way from the

Sattyn-Whiley box down to the grand lobby in search of whoever had summoned him. He had no idea what it was all about, but, truth to tell, he really didn't mind at all being called away from his Sattyn-Whiley box.

"Dr. Sattyn-Whiley?" an usher asked. He was a venerable gentleman whose purplish-veined nose told Dr. Sattyn-Whiley's trained eye that he had for years been rather overfond of the grape.

"Yes," Dr. Sattyn-Whiley replied.

"Come with me, please, Doctor," the usher said. He led Dr. Sattyn-Whiley back into the building, through a corridor running parallel to the auditorium, and then held a door open for him.

"Good luck, Doc," the usher said. "You'll need it."

He found himself in a small room containing an octagonal table covered with what appeared to be an army blanket. There was only one person in the room —a tall, red-headed, ruddy-faced chap attired in white tie and tails.

"Do you know who I am, Cornie?" the man asked.

"Yes, sir," Dr. Sattyn-Whiley replied. "But only by reputation."

"At the risk of challenging all that you hold near and dear, Cornie," the man said, "there are times when a boy should not listen to his momma."

"Oh, I don't mean that, sir," Dr. Sattyn-Whiley replied. "I mean the Bergerhorn-Grogarty Upper-Bowel Bypass."*

"You're familiar with that?"

"Oh, yes, sir," Dr. Sattyn-Whiley said. "I've been privileged to learn the technique."

"That was one of Ferdie's better ideas," the man said. "But I wasn't talking of medicine, Cornie. I

---

* Dr. Sattyn-Whiley here referred to a surgical technique devised by Doctors Aloysius J. Grogarty and J. Ferdinand Bergerhorn for treatment of the chronically obese. Briefly, it consists of hooking the bowel to the upper quarter of the stomach, thus cutting off the lower three-quarters of the stomach from the ingestion-digestion process. The fatties can thus eat all they want, but all they want, following the procedure, is about twenty-five percent of what they wanted, preprocedure.

meant to ask if you know who I *am*, and what our relationship is."

"Well, you, sir, are Aloysius J. Grogarty, M.D., F.A.C.S., and chief of staff of the Grogarty Clinic."

"More important than that," Dr. Grogarty replied, "I am your godfather. Before your birth, your father and I were the best of friends. There was an unfortunate understanding with your mother. . . ."

"Don't you mean 'misunderstanding,' sir?"

"No, I do not," Dr. Grogarty said. "Your mother and I understand each other perfectly. But despite that, the fact remains that I am your godfather and have certain responsibilities to you, especially now that you're about to enter the doctor business."*

"I had hoped, when the time was right, to ask my father to introduce me to you, sir," Dr. Sattyn-Whiley said.

"You would have waited a long time, I fear," Dr. Grogarty said, his voice level. "Your father is an obedient husband."

"Well, in any event," Dr. Sattyn-Whiley said, "whatever medical emergency has arisen tonight, it has at least given me the privilege of meeting you. And speaking of the medical emergency, how can I be of assistance to you, Doctor?"

"There is no medical emergency," Dr. Grogarty said. "You were summoned here tonight, Cornie, for two reasons: first, that you are my godson, and second, that you are rich. It has also come to my attention, via the medical grapevine, that when you were at that establishment on the banks of the Charles, you sometimes whiled away the idle hours at a game of chance known as poker."

At that moment, the door from the corridor opened

---

* As a matter of information, it should be noted that Dr. Grogarty had discreetly used a good deal of his considerable influence to have Dr. Sattyn-Whiley accepted as a surgical resident at that unnamed medical facility on the banks of the Charles River. He had taken this action in the realization that because of his relationship with Mrs. C. Edward Sattyn-Whiley, Dr. Sattyn-Whiley could not serve his residency in the Grogarty Clinic, and the second-best facility would have to do.

and Colonel C. Edward Whiley stepped into the room.

"Dad!" Dr. Sattyn-Whiley said.

"Hello, Irish," Colonel Whiley said. "I hope I'm welcome."

"How are you, Charley?" Dr. Grogarty replied. "Frankly, you look awful."

"I asked if I'm welcome," Colonel Whiley said.

"You're welcome," Dr. Grogarty replied. "That's a steel door, strong enough to repel even your enraged wife. But what are you going to do about her later?"

"I'll handle that when I get to it," Colonel Whiley said.

"How did you know where we were?" Grogarty asked.

"Irish, for twenty-five years, every time the conductor raises his baton to begin the overture, number thirteen has flashed on the callboard and you've left your seat."

"You noticed that, did you?"

"And tonight, when the conductor raised his baton and number thirteen flashed on, followed by number one, I realized that I had a choice to make. Either I could stay in my seat from now on, while you and my son were playing poker, or I could join you. Or at least I could ask to join you."

"What did you tell the old battle—Caroline?"

"I told her that I was having stomach trouble," the colonel said.

"Lying to your wife, I am told, is a sin. But not in this case, Charley, right?"

"What do you mean?"

"You can stay on one condition," Dr. Grogarty said. "I want to see you in my office at half-past eight in the morning. I wasn't kidding before. You look like death warmed over."

"There's nothing—"

"You see that he's there, Doctor," Dr. Grogarty said. "You understand me?"

"Yes, sir," Dr. Sattyn-Whiley said.

"Two against one, Charley," Dr. Grogarty said. "What do you say?"

"I'll be there," Colonel Whiley said.

"Well, then, sit down. I hope you brought lots of money."

"Who else is playing?" Colonel Whiley said. "I haven't played in twenty-five years."

"I know," Dr. Grogarty said. "That's not all you haven't been doing, either."

The door at the opposite end of the room opened and J. Robespierre O'Reilly and His Royal Highness the Sheikh of Abzug, together with two of His Highness' bodyguards, walked into the room.

"Sorry to be late," J. Robespierre O'Reilly said, "but pumpkin always likes me to stay backstage until she goes on."

"Sit down, Radar," Dr. Grogarty said, "and shut up and deal." He turned to Dr. Sattyn-Whiley. "Take his pulse, Cornie," said Dr. Grogarty, indicating His Royal Highness, "and give him one of these." He threw Dr. Sattyn-Whiley a Tums for the tummy. "That way you can truthfully tell your mother that you were summoned to treat His Royal Highness for stomach distress."

His Royal Highness seemed a little confused about having his wrist held and being given the foil-wrapped medication. Radar explained what was going on. His Royal Highness reached up and pinched Dr. Sattyn-Whiley on the cheek.

"What's this?" Dr. Sattyn-Whiley inquired.

"Oh, from the looks of it, about three carats," Radar said. "The one he just gave Kris was a little bigger."

His Royal Highness sat down at the table.

"Deal the cards!" he said. "His nibs is hot tonight!"

Chapter Two

"Spruce Harbor Medical Center," the switchboard operator of that medical facility said, after she had pushed the appropriate button.

"Dr. Aloysius J. Grogarty of the Grogarty Clinic for Dr. Benjamin Franklin Pierce," a precise voice announced. "And please stand by for the transmission of EKG and x-ray."

Despite what some of its critics alleged, the Spruce Harbor Medical Center was a well-equipped institution, fully capable of both receiving and transmitting, via quite clever and very expensive machines, electrocardiograms and x-ray photographs. It had, in fact, the very latest and most expensive equipment, which had been presented to the medical center some three months before by Mr. Wayne Lussey, chairman of the board of the Spruce Harbor Building & Loan Association, as a small gesture of his affection and respect for Dr. Pierce, the Spruce Harbor chief of surgery, and all the other medical practitioners of the institution.

Mr. Lussey, who had attended a savings-and-loan chief executives' association convention in Mexico City while his wife was off on a three-month around-the-world-tour, had returned with a little souvenir of the convention. It was not, however, the sort of souvenir that he would (or could) display on his mantelpiece to recall a happy moment in his life, and certainly not the sort of souvenir he would wish Mrs. Lussey to even hear about.

When his souvenir was first diagnosed by Dr. Pierce, in fact, Mr. Lussey was reluctant to admit that anything of that sort could possibly happen to him.

"Hawkeye," he'd said, in high indignation, "you don't mean it!"

"You are speaking, sir," Dr. Pierce had replied, "to the former social-disease-control officer of the 4077th Mobile Army Surgical Hospital, fondly remembered as the Double Natural MASH. I know a dose of—"

"Don't say it!" Mr. Lussey had hastily interrupted.

"When I see one," Dr. Pierce had gone on. "Whatever are you going to say to Mrs. Lussey when she returns home from her tour of the world's cultural capitals and places like that?"

"Isn't there anything that can be done?"

"My diagnosis might possibly be in error," Dr. Pierce had said. "You could do one of two things. You could seek another opinion. I know a good G&S man in Bangor. . . ."

"G&S?"

"Gonorrh—"

"You said two things," Mr. Lussey had said quickly. "What was the other?"

"Well, as I said, my diagnosis might be in error."

"It might?"

"There's only one way I could tell for sure whether you have what I think you have or whether it's merely an advanced case of athlete's foot."

"*Athlete's* foot?"

"By an odd coincidence, the treatment for a severe case of athlete's foot, such as you might possibly have, is just about the same thing . . . massive doses of penicillin . . . as it is for that other unmentionable social condition."

"It is?"

"Indeed. And I recall a case quite clearly where a chap who had both was cured of both at the same time."

"You don't say?" Mr. Lussey had said. "I probably

caught it at the Spruce Harbor Health Spa. How soon can you start treatment?"

"That poses a little problem," Dr. Pierce had said. "I won't know if it's athlete's foot until I run some tests, and our present testing equipment is so old that I consider it unreliable."

"Then get some new equipment," Mr. Lussey had said. "I'll pay for it!"

"I thought you'd say that. I just happen to have some literature here in my desk." Dr. Pierce had opened the drawer and pushed some four-color brochures across his desk to the savings-and-loan executive.

Mr. Lussey had examined it briefly.

"This doesn't say anything about athlete's foot," he'd said. "This equipment is an expensive data transmission system. What sort of data do you have to transmit about athlete's foot?"

"I sometimes like to seek outside opinions on really bad cases of what you have," Dr. Pierce had said.

"Athlete's foot, you mean," Mr. Lussey had said.

"We won't know that until we have the equipment, will we?" Dr. Pierce had countered.

"But it costs $21,750!"

"The G&S man's name is Carter, but they call him Old Blabbermouth," Dr. Pierce had said. "He holds office hours every day. I'll give him a call and make an appointment for you—"

Mr. Lussey had gotten his checkbook out and begun to scribble furiously.

"You're a good man, Mr. Lussey," Dr. Pierce had said, taking the check from him and blowing on it, "with the interests of your fellow citizens always at heart. Now drop your pants and sort of lean over my desk."

And so it came to pass that the Spruce Harbor Medical facility had as good a data transmission system as could be expected under the circumstances. And there was no reason why the Spruce Harbor Medical Center in Maine could not stand by for the transmission of x-ray photographs, EKGs, and other medical data from the Grogarty Clinic all the way across the continent in San Francisco. Indeed, the operator immediately pushed the buttons that would permit such data transmission.

The other part of the request, that Dr. Grogarty be permitted to speak with Dr. Pierce, did pose a problem. A little blue light above Dr. Pierce's button on the switchboard was illuminated, signifying that Dr. Pierce was in conference.

Dr. Pierce had, in fact, been in conference since half-past four. With him were Dr. John Francis Xavier McIntyre, a fellow Fellow of the American College of Surgeons; Esther Flanagan, R.N., chief of nursing services and head operating-room nurse at the medical center, and Miss Barbara Jane Miller, an about-to-graduate student nurse.

It had been a full day in the medical center's surgical suite, with both a heavy load of previously scheduled surgery and an extraordinary amount of emergency surgery.

The operator knew that it was Dr. Pierce's custom in such circumstances to repair to his offices, together with those who had worked with him, to review what had taken place on the operating table, and, as he put it, to "unwind a bit." When Dr. Pierce was in conference (the operator thought of it as "when the warning light was lit)," he did not like to be disturbed. As a matter of fact, he violently objected to being disturbed in any event save the most pressing medical emergency and had frequently demonstrated a rather violent burst of temper when his conferences had been interrupted by what he considered unimportant matters.

Therefore, the operator said to the Grogarty Clinic operator, "Spruce Harbor Medical Center is ready to receive your data, but I regret that Dr. Pierce is in conference and cannot be disturbed."

"One moment please, operator," Grogarty Clinic said. There was a pause and then she came back on the line. "We are now beginning the transmission of data." There was another pause, and then the Spruce Harbor operator spoke.

"The data transmission is operating satisfactorily," she reported.

"Dr. Grogarty advises that in the event Dr. Pierce is in conference and not available, he will speak with Dr. John F. X. McIntyre."

"I'm sorry, operator," the Spruce Harbor operator said, "but Dr. McIntyre is also in conference. I'll have him call when he is free."

"One moment, please, operator," the Grogarty Clinic operator said.

And then another voice, a male voice, came on the line.

"This is Dr. Grogarty," he said. His voice sort of boomed. "You say that Dr. Pierce and Dr. McIntyre are both in conference?"

"Yes, sir."

"Is it possible that they are in conference *together?*"

"Yes, Doctor."

"And is this conference being conducted in Dr. Pierce's chief of surgery's office?"

"Yes, Doctor, it is," the operator said.

"Well, then, honey," Dr. Grogarty boomed, "you get either Hawkeye* or Trapper John** on the line and tell them to put down the gin and pick up the phone 'cause Aloysius J. Grogarty's on the other end of the line and the boozing will just have to wait."

Stunned that the caller actually knew what was

---

* Dr. Pierce's father was a great fan of James Fenimore Cooper, and in particular of his monumental work, *The Last of the Mohicans.* Although he could not convince his wife that their first-born should be so christened, he had never called his eldest son anything but Hawkeye, and as time passed only Dr. Pierce's mother, the U.S. Army, and the Maine State Board for the Licensing of Medical Practitioners had continued to insist on calling him by the name on his birth certificate.

** While a college student in Maine, Dr. McIntyre had been discovered, *deshabille,* as they say, and *en flagrante delicto,* with a coed in the gentlemen's rest facility aboard a Boston & Maine Railroad train. With shocking disregard for the facts and with her eye on her reputation, his lady friend, the moment the door had been jerked open on them, had announced that he had "trapped her" in the room. From that moment on, John Francis Xavier McIntyre had been known to friend and foe alike as "Trapper John."

going on in Dr. Pierce's office, the operator pressed the button that caused the telephone to ring on his desk.

When the telephone rang, Dr. Pierce, Dr. McIntyre, Nurse Flanagan, and Student Nurse Miller, still dressed in their surgical greens, were bent over a table in the office. Doctors Pierce and McIntyre each held large hypodermic syringes with large-size needles, and each was, with infinite care and great skill, depressing the plunger of his syringe. What would have struck the casual observer of this otherwise fairly routine medical procedure was that what they were injecting something into the soles of a pair of golf shoes.

Therein, as they say, lies a tale.

Hawkeye Pierce and Trapper John McIntyre were, as they frequently admitted, indeed boasted, "two guys who could certainly hold a grudge."

One of those against whom the healers, former military surgeons and honorary Knights Commander of the Bayou Perdu (La.) Council, Knights of Columbus, held a long-standing grudge was Francis Burns, M.D., of Hillandale, Ohio.

Their grudge against Dr. Burns was of the active, rather than latent, variety. That is to say, they didn't merely harbor a resentful memory of Dr. Burns, idly hoping for the day when Lady Luck would put them in a position to, for example, let the air out of his tires on a rainy night. No, their grudge was of the active variety, and they gave some thought to and received a great deal of pleasure from zinging Frank Burns whenever possible.

And lest time start to heal the wounds, lest they be tempted to put all that Frank Burns had done to them beyond them, as water over the dam, they kept a sort of a memorial to Dr. Burns in Dr. Pierce's office. At no small cost, they had had a photograph of Dr. Burns, taken during the Korean Unpleasantness, converted into a dart board.

It had been *Major* Burns then—or as the Army insists on putting it, Burns, Francis, Major, Medical Corps (as it been Pierce, Benjamin F., Captain, Medical Corps, and McIntyre, J. F. X., Captain, Medical Corps). And therein had been the germ of the problem. Majors are not only permitted but are actually encouraged by the military establishment to give orders to captains. It was not that Captains Pierce and McIntyre had objected to taking orders from their betters. They had, in fact, regularly taken orders from the hospital commander, Lieutenant Colonel Henry Blake, Medical Corps, U.S. Army.*

What Hawkeye and Trapper John had had trouble doing *vis à vis* Francis Burns, M.D., when they were all assigned to the 4077th Mobile Army Surgical Hospital in the Iron Triangle of Korea, had been accepting the Army's and Major Burns' notion that Dr. Burns was a surgeon. Neither Captain Pierce nor Captain McIntyre, M.C., U.S.A., were very much impressed by Dr. Burns' tailored and stiffly starched surgical greens (complete with insignia of rank on both shoulders).

"It takes more than surgical greens, no matter how well tailored, to make a surgeon," as Dr. Pierce had said.

"Starting with knowing which end of the scalpel to hold," Dr. McIntyre had agreed.

In private practice, it had not been at all hard to find out. Dr. Burns had been proprietor of a thriving pediatric clinic, where his surgery had been essentially limited to extracting large sums of money from first-time mothers by agreeing with their every dark and imaginative suspicion regarding their children's health. On those rare occasions when it had been impossible to find a nurse with free time on her hands to remove a splinter from the hand of one of his prepubescent patients and Dr. Burns' personal services had been required, he had proved so inept that—privately,

---

* Colonel Blake, despite irresponsible reports to the contrary from people who would have known better had they been able to read words of more than one syllable, survived the Korean War and achieved high rank. A rather touching, and certainly splendidly written, account of his faithful service to his country as sort of a medical diplomat (and major general) may be found in *M*A*S*H Goes to Paris* (Pocket Books, New York). This tome is a real bargain at a buck and a half.

of course—his fellow medical practitioners had referred to him as "The Bumbling Baby Butcher of Shady Lane."

How it had come to pass no one knew, but while passing through the Army's school for newly commissioned doctors, Frank Burns had been classified as a surgeon. There were several theories of how this had happened, ranging from a hung-over clerk punching a hole in the wrong place on the IBM card to the theory to which Doctors Pierce and McIntyre subscribed: that the North Koreans had infiltrated a secret agent into the medical training center, where, by assigning inept clowns like Frank Burns as frontline surgeons, he stood a good chance of killing off more troops than the North Korean Army would on the battlefield.

Major Burns' surgical ineptitude had been known to Colonel Blake, who had been, in the opinion of Doctors Pierce and McIntyre, a fair-to-middling cutter himself. Wise in the ways of the Army, Colonel Blake had, before Doctors Pierce and McIntyre arrived in Korea, done two things to keep Burns from wiping out the corps of patients. He had appointed Burns his deputy commander, in full charge of such military necessities as giving the "Why We Are Fighting Here" and "How To Avoid Social Disease" lectures; counting the Hershey bars in the PX; and making sure that all the Jeeps had a wheel at each corner. He was also named the morale officer, the VD-control officer, the officers'-club officer, the postal officer, and the re-enlistment officer.

Colonel Blake had also had a word with Major Margaret Houlihan, Army Nurse Corps, a veteran professional soldier herself and a fine operating-room nurse. Major Houlihan had been told, soldier to soldier, that Major Burns was not to be allowed to perform any surgery of a complexity greater than trimming a fingernail unless every other doctor had fallen *hors de combat*.*

---

* This little G.I. *tête-à-tête* resulted in a slight misunderstanding at first. Major Houlihan, who, as the senior nurse, felt a firm loyalty to her

After the arrival of Captains Hawkeye Pierce and Trapper John McIntyre at the 4077th MASH, other problems developed. Colonel Blake had quickly come to understand that his two new surgeons were (a) splendid surgeons and (b) lousy officers, at least when judged by the standards of Major Francis Burns, who had, upon donning his first uniform at the reception center, instantly come to think of himself as the George S. Patton of the Medical Corps.

As he frequently pointed out to Colonel Blake, his being referred to as "Old Bumble Fingers," "El Bedpan," and "Hèy, you!" violated every known canon of military courtesy and discipline.

Forced to choose between maintaining military discipline and providing his patients with the best cutters available, Colonel Blake had flown (perhaps "flapped" would be a better word) in the face of tradition and appointed Captain Hawkeye Pierce as chief surgeon of the 4077th MASH and Captain Trapper John McIntyre as his deputy.

With two exceptions this appointment pleased the entire medical staff of the 4077th MASH.

Major Burns was annoyed, of course. It was quite clear to him that since he was a major he knew more about any given subject, including surgery, than any lowly captain, and thus the appointment should have been his. He brought this logical conclusion to the attention of Colonel Blake at his first opportunity, and Colonel Blake responded with the succinct phraseology of command for which the career soldier is famous.

"Shut up, Frank," Colonel Blake had replied. "And get your fat ass out of my tent."

Tears had come to Major Burns' eyes, and as he had marched out of Colonel Blake's tent his somewhat obscured vision had caused him to bump into Major Margaret Houlihan.

***

subordinates, was not fluent in French. "If your doctors, Colonel," she said, "are fooling around, they're not fooling around with my nurses. Bite your tongue, sir!"

Although Major Houlihan was not only a first-class nurse but a professional soldier as well, under her 38 D chest beat, of course, the heart of woman, and women, as a class, manifest on occasion an emotion known as the maternal instinct. This maternal emotion burst into full bloom in Major Houlihan's bosom the moment she saw Frank Burns' face with a tear running down each cheek.

She knew that this man, this boyish chap, this tall fellow who alone among the officer-doctors of the 4077th MASH had observed every subtle nuance of the correct interofficer relationship (he had, in other words, always referred to her as "Major" Houlihan, rather than as "Nurse," or "Hey, you!"), had just suffered some unbearable (and probably unspeakable) tribulation, and that it behooved her as both woman and fellow major to console him in his hour of pain.

Major Margaret Houlihan accomplished this by taking Major Frank Burns to her tent, giving him a couple of belts of medicinal bourbon, and encouraging him, as one officer to another, to open his heart to her.

Possibly it was because he was so distressed by the gross injustice of what had happened to him that Major Burns, in relating to Major Houlihan the story of his life, neglected to mention that there was at home a Mrs. Francis Burns and four little Burnses.

One thing, as they say, led to another, starting with Major Houlihan's professional medical opinion that if two ounces of medicinal bourbon had made Major Burns stop crying, four would probably make him smile. To cut a long and somewhat sordid story short, when reveille sounded the next morning, it found Major Burns and Major Houlihan in flagrant violation of a military regulation themselves. The Army frowns on two officers sharing the same cot, folding, field, wood and canvas, M1917A2, and, in fact, strictly proscribes such behavior.

"This is bigger than both of us, Frank!" Major Margaret Houlihan had cried.

"Not much bigger," Major Frank Burns had replied. "I almost fell out."

"I mean our love!" she'd said.

"Oh," he'd replied. "If you say so, Margaret."*

Major Houlihan, just as soon as she got dressed, brought the matter of the unjust appointment of Captain Hawkeye Pierce to the position of chief surgeon up to Colonel Blake.

"As one soldier to another, Colonel," Major Houlihan said, "it is obviously a gross miscarriage of military justice!"

"As one soldier to another, Major," Colonel Blake had responded, "I am surprised that you have forgotten that basic philosophy upon which the military services function."

"I beg your pardon, sir?"

"The colonel may not always be right, Major, but he's always the colonel," Colonel Blake said. "Sometimes expressed as 'Yours is not to reason why, Major, yours is but to do what you're told to do without sticking your nose in where it's not wanted.' You read me?"

Major Houlihan that night was consoled by Major Burns, and vice versa. The next day, which happened to be her day off, Major Houlihan did something she remained ashamed of for the rest of her life. (It had nothing to do, for those with an all-consuming prurient interest who are still with us, with her amoro-biological relationship with Major Burns.

What she did—blinded both by love and the rest of the half-gallon of medicinal bourbon—was to "go over Colonel Blake's head." Specifically, she journeyed by Jeep to Eighth Army Headquarters in Seoul and brought the unjust appointment of Captains Pierce

---

* It is not the authors' intention to dwell on the Burns-Houlihan affair. For those with a prurient interest in such things, the details have been recorded in *M*A*S*H*, which Pocket Books, as their contribution to *belle lettres*, has seen fit to make available to the general public via the better bus-station, airport, and drug-store paperback racks at a very nominal price of $1.50.

and McIntyre to the positions of chief surgeon and deputy chief surgeon, respectively, to the attention of the Eighth Army surgeon.

As that dignitary chased her around his desk, urging her to lie down and talk about it, it occurred to him that perhaps there was something to what Major Houlihan was saying beyond the fact that her new boyfriend's feelings had been hurt.

For one thing, he knew Major Houlihan to be a fine operating-room nurse. He had personally chased her around G.I. operating rooms from the Panama Canal Zone to Alaska and had seen her at work. For another, it wasn't a good idea to appoint junior officers to positions that should be occupied by more senior officers.

He told her that he would "look into it." He looked into it two ways. He telephoned Colonel Blake and just happened to mention it to him. He was shocked by Colonel Blake's response. Colonel Blake, previously a fine officer, told the Eighth Army surgeon that if he didn't like the way he was running the 4077th MASH, the Eighth Army surgeon knew into which orifice of the body he could stuff it.

"I'm overworked and understaffed," Blake went on. "And if you want to help me, Sammy, you can get off the phone, get up here, scrub, and grab a scalpel. Otherwise, bug off!"

And with that, the commanding officer of the 4077th MASH hung up on the surgeon of the Eighth United States Army.

Three hours later, the Eighth Army surgeon arrived by helicopter at the 4077th MASH, wholly prepared to relieve Colonel Blake of his command and to place Major Burns, as ranking officer, in command, at least temporarily.

He was informed that the entire medical staff of the 4077th MASH was in the operating room. The Eighth Army surgeon scrubbed, put on surgical greens, and entered the operating room.

At the first table, two surgeons were in the process of removing pieces of shrapnel from the intestinal cavity of a young soldier. The taller of them looked up quickly, saw the newcomer, and then dropped his eyes back to his work.

"I suppose it's too much to hope, Chubby," he said, "that you're a surgeon?"

"As it happens," the Eighth Army surgeon replied, somewhat testily, "I am."

"The term is bandied about somewhat loosely in these parts," the tall chap said. "But I'm desperate and have to take the chance. Close this guy up. I've got one waiting that's in just about as bad shape."

The Eighth Army surgeon realized that he had just been ordered around like an intern by one of his very junior subordinates. But as the junior surgeon stepped away from the table, he stepped up to it.

"What have we got here?" he asked the other surgeon.

"He doesn't know," the departing surgeon called over his shoulder. "That's Dago Red. He's the chaplain."

"I try to help as best I can," the man whom the Eighth Army surgeon had thought was a doctor said.

The Eighth Army surgeon bent over the table.

Four hours later, as he finished closing a badly torn leg, the Eighth Army surgeon looked up and found the eyes of the tall young man on him.

"You're pretty good with that knife, Chubby," he said. "And we're glad to have you. Come on down to the swamp and have a martini with us."

Still in his soiled surgical clothing, the Eighth Army surgeon walked to the most disreputable tent he had ever seen in twenty-five years of military service. While a full inventory of the tent beggars description, suffice it to say that the beds showed no evidence whatever of ever having been made, that an anatomical skeleton dressed in a bikini stood in one corner smoking a cigar, and that a still bubbled merrily in another corner.

He accepted a martini, which filled the eight-ounce glass in which it was served, took one appreciative sip, and then slumped into the chrome-and-leather barber's chair the tall young doctor offered him. He took another sip of the martini and found that both young doctors were smiling at him.

"Martini all right?" the taller one asked.

"Just fine," the Eighth Army surgeon said.

"Cold enough? Not too much vermouth?"

"Just fine," the Eighth Army surgeon repeated.

"Been in the Army long, have you?" the tall one inquired.

"Long enough," the Eighth Army surgeon replied.

"Would it be safe, then, to presume you're higher-ranking than a captain?" the tall one asked.

"Yes, you could say that," the Eighth Army surgeon, who was a brigadier general, replied.

"Maybe even higher than a major?" the shorter one asked.

"You could say that, too," the general said.

At that point, the man whom the Eighth Army surgeon had met at the operating table came into the tent. He was wordlessly offered and wordlessly accepted a martini. He was wearing the insignia of a chaplain, and captain's bars.

"Dago Red," the tall one said, "you've met the new guy, haven't you?"

"Not officially," the chaplain said. "I'm Father Mulcahy," he said, putting out his hand to the Eighth Army surgeon. "Do you happen to be a Catholic?"

"No, I don't," the Eighth Army surgeon replied.

"No matter," Father Mulcahy said. "Welcome anyway."

"I didn't get the name, Chubby," the tall one said. "You've already met Dago Red, and this is Trapper John McIntyre, and I'm Hawkeye Pierce."

"My friends call me Sammy," the Eighth Army surgeon said.

At that point, Colonel Blake, who had been advised by his clerk, Corporal J. Robespierre "Radar" O'Reilly, that the Eighth Army surgeon was in the hospital area, came into the tent. Because of the merrily bubbling still, which blocked his view, he could not see the occupant of the barber chair.

34

"I'm going to lay an order on you guys," the colonel said. "And for once, you'd damned well better obey it."

Doctors Pierce and McIntyre immediately dropped to their knees and bowed three times, in the manner of Moslems at prayer.

"We hear and obey, O Worshipful Master!" they cried in unison.

"I'm serious," Colonel Blake said.

"I'm Hawkeye," said Hawkeye.

"Look, I blew my cool this morning and told the Eighth Army surgeon to stick the MASH up . . . you know where."

"Give the man a martini," Trapper John said. "How brave of you, Colonel!"

"And he's here!" Colonel Blake went on. "I'm in enough trouble without him seeing you. So you guys stay in the tent until further orders. You read me?"

"What were you being beastly to the Eighth Army surgeon *about*, Henry?" Hawkeye asked.

"Frank Burns," the colonel said. "Somebody told him I had named you chief surgeon over him."

"Your problems, O Maximum Leader," Trapper John said, "are over!"

"What the hell are you talking about?"

"The Eighth Army surgeon has finally done something right," Hawkeye said. "He sent us a cutter who is actually a cutter, not a refugee from a chiropractor's clinic. This guy is actually a better cutter than me, as hard as you may find that to believe."

"Not only that," Trapper John joined in, "but he's higher in rank than Frank Burns. So you just name *him* chief surgeon, and the flap is unflapped. It's as simple as that."

"What the hell are you talking about?" Colonel Blake demanded.

"Sammy, stand up and salute and meet the boss. He's big on G.I. crap like saluting and standing up straight."

Colonel Blake peered around the merrily bubbling still just in time to see the Eighth Army surgeon rising from the barber chair.

35

"Nice little place you've got here, Henry," the Eighth Army surgeon said. "A little odd, perhaps, but you've got one hell of a fine chief of surgery."

"I, uh, didn't expect to see you here, Sam," Colonel Blake said.

"Well, you said that if I wanted to help I should come up here, scrub, and grab a scalpel," the Eighth Army surgeon said. "So I did."

"I gather you know each other?" Hawkeye said. "That's even better."

"I've got bad news for you, Slim," the Eighth Army surgeon said.

"You can call me Hawkeye, Chubby," Hawkeye replied.

"And you can call me General, Hawkeye," the general said. "And as I was saying, I've got bad news for you. You're stuck as chief of surgery here. You can consider it a permanent assignment." He started for the door.

"You're not leaving?" Colonel Blake asked.

"I have to have a word with Major Houlihan," the general said. "And then I'll be going back to Seoul."

The word he had with Major Houlihan he had in private, of course, and, truth to tell, both Hawkeye and Trapper John had naughty thoughts about what was really going on behind the closed door of Major Houlihan's tent. . . .

Speaking as soldier to soldier, the Eighth Army surgeon told the chief nurse of the 4077th MASH that the only reason he wasn't shipping her home in disgrace was because she was a good operating-room nurse and was needed at the 4077th.

"Think what you like about those two clowns with the private still and the barber's chair, Margaret," he said, "they're first-class surgeons, and that's the bottom line. I had a moment or two to observe that simpering jackass, Frank Burns, at work on the table, and my first reaction was to have him sent home on the next plane. The only reason I'm not doing that is because he'd love it, and, more important, if I keep him here, he can empty bedpans, sweep the floor, give social-disease shots, and free the enlisted men for more important things."

"I'm sorry, Sammy," Margaret said. "I really am."

"Soldier to soldier, Major," the general said, "you're blinded by love for that jackass."

"You really think so?" she asked, on the verge of tears.

"You can take it from me, Major," the general said. "I'm a doctor, and we know all about things like that."

"What should I do?"

"I thought you'd never ask," the general said. "You keep that jackass out of Colonel Blake's hair, and you keep him out of Hawkeye and Trapper John's hair."

"Yes, sir," Major Houlihan said, snapping to attention and saluting. Saluting required that she raise her right hand (with the arm attached, of course) so that the extended fingers touched her eyebrow. As she raised her arm, the pectoral muscles grew taut, lifting those organs contained in what the quartermaster general referred to as "Container, bosoms, with harness, heavy duty, winter and summer, M1940B4, size 38 D" into a rather spectacular position.

The general's mouth dropped open. It was all too clear what Major Burns saw in Major Houlihan, although what *she* saw in *him* he couldn't imagine.

"Carry on, Major," he finally snapped, and then marched out of her tent, went back to his helicopter, and flew back to Seoul.

Despite her good intentions, Major Houlihan was not able to restrain the emotions in her magnificent bosom. In the operating room, she was as quick as anyone else to block Frank Burns' way whenever it appeared that he might be approaching one of the patients with surgery in mind. But if it wasn't quite literally a matter of life and death—in other words, *out* of the operating room—her emotions got the best of her. Whenever she laid her soft brown eyes on Frank Burns' bewildered little boy's face, whenever she saw the hurt in his eyes after one of the others (truth to tell, usually Hawkeye or Trapper John) had hurt his sensitive feelings by some masculine cruelty, the desire to wrap him in her arms and comfort him swelled up in her bosom and overcame logic and common sense.

It must be admitted, too, that neither Dr. Pierce nor Dr. McIntyre were entirely blameless in the matter; their conduct was certainly (and admittedly) not that expected of officers and gentlemen of the Army Medical Corps.

An officer and a gentleman, for example, would not dream of rigging the nurses' shower tent wall so that it would come tumbling down while the chief nurse was at her morning ablutions. This happened, to Major Houlihan's obvious discomfiture and the great glee of the ambulatory ward, while said ambulatory patients "happened" to be walking by.

And it took the exact antithesis of an officer and a gentleman to conceive, much less execute, the foul idea of placing the microphone to the hospital public-address system under the springs of Major Houlihan's cot, so that the entire hospital became privy to the most intimate of discussions between that officer and gentlewoman and Major Burns.*

Major Houlihan and Major Burns remained the best of friends for about six months. (The friendship ended when Major Houlihan became aware that Mrs. Frank Burns and the four little Burnses back in Hillandale, Ohio, were a fact, not just another scurrilous rumor spread by Doctors Pierce and McIntyre. But that is another, somewhat sordid story, on which we will not dwell.)

During that six-month period, Hot Lips remembered afterwards with remorse and chagrin, she was Frank Burns' willing partner in what Major Burns referred to as "straightening this circus out."

---

* During this incident, shortly before cheers, whistles, and applause announced that they were not quite as alone as they had presumed, Major Burns told Major Houlihan that her lips burned like a holy fire. When Major Houlihan stuck her head out of the tent to ascertain the cause of the cheers, whistles, and applause, Captain Pierce cried out, "Here she is, gang! Let's hear it! Three cheers for Hot Lips Houlihan!" For some reason, the unfortunate appellation stuck.

While Colonel Blake was physically on the premises, of course, nothing toward that end could be accomplished, for Colonel Blake apparently preferred what Major Burns thought of as a three-ring circus to a G.I. MASH. But the moment the colonel's Jeep passed out of sight down the dirt road to the main supply route, Major Frank Burns, by the Army's immutable laws of seniority, became the hospital commander.

And as hospital commander, his powers *vis à vis* saluting, reveille, shining boots, and performing that quaint choreography known as close-order drill were limitless, at least so far as the enlisted men were concerned—which is why he came to be held in such passionate loathing by Hawkeye and Trapper John.

The very first morning Major Burns found himself hospital commander *pro tem,* he appeared at the bachelor officers' quarters occupied by Captains Pierce and McIntyre. Major Houlihan had provided him with a brass whistle, which he blew immediately upon entering the tent.

"All right, men!" he cried, in creditable mimicry of the sergeant who had conducted the medical officer's indoctrination program at Fort Sam Houston. "Let's hit it!"

"You blow that whistle again, pig-eyes," Dr. Pierce responded, "and I'll make you eat it!"

"You officers are in charge of this morning's close-order drill!" Major Burns said. "Hop to it!"

In perfect duet, Captains Pierce and McIntyre suggested that Major Burns perform a physiologically impossible act of attempted self-impregnation.

"What did you say?" he asked, shocked to the quick.

Both doctors repeated the suggestion, this time pronouncing each syllable with great clarity, so there would be no chance whatsoever that they would be misunderstood.

"You just wait till I tell the colonel what you said!" Major Burns said, fleeing the tent. "He'll fix you!"

Despite the threat (which he indeed carried out), Major Burns was momentarily frustrated. Under similar circumstances, he would take his problem to Major Houlihan, who, drawing upon her greater military experience, would tell him what subsequent steps to take. But he could not take this defiance of his legal authority to Major Houlihan, for that would mean repeating verbatim what Hawkeye and Trapper John had told him to do, and Frank Burns had been told by his mother never to use language like that in the presence of a lady.

So he himself conducted close-order drill for the enlisted men. This posed an awful problem for Doctors Pierce and McIntyre. While they found the idea of marching to and fro to Frank Burns' somewhat nasal orders repulsive, the idea that the troops should be doing it, with equal reluctance, while they hid behind their officer status and relative immunity, was even more repugnant. So, attired in a blanket (Dr. Pierce) and a silk dressing gown (Dr. McIntyre), Hawkeye and Trapper John, muttering naughty words not very much under their breath, joined the enlisted men.

It only happened that once. (During that night, party or parties unknown burned all of Major Burns' footwear; it being difficult, if not absolutely impossible to march on a rocky field in one's bare feet, close-order drill was temporarily abandoned.) But once was enough, and close-order drill was not the only means by which Major Burns attempted to infiltrate what he thought of as "soldierly behavior" into the 4077th MASH. Because the enlisted men's mess (which also served as their recreation center) did not meet Major Burns' Pattonesque standards of neatness and decorum, he (a) tore down and burned what Doctors Pierce and McIntyre regarded as one of the finest displays of pulchritudinous art in Korea and (b) suspended the sale of beer.

Providing the troops with a wee drop with which to water down their cares was simply a matter of operating the still on a twenty-four-hour (rather than an eight-hour) basis, but the enlisted men's art gallery was lost forever, and that was obviously unforgivable.

When Colonel Blake returned from his business in Seoul and opposing sides brought what they considered to be statements of misbehavior on the part of others to his attention, the colonel, although his sympathies clearly lay with the troops and Trapper John and Hawkeye, was placed in a somewhat delicate position.

While he did not condone the shutting off of the troops' beer and the destruction of the art gallery, neither could he condone all-night drinking parties in bachelor officers' quarters by the troops. And while he did think that, as fellow officers of the command, Captains Pierce and McIntyre had had every right to give Major Burns the benefit of their thinking *vis à vis* the enlisted men's morale, he had to agree with Major Burns that being called a "miserable chicken-bleep son of a blap" by Captains Pierce and McIntyre did go a bit beyond the language permitted for officers when addressing a superior.

What Major Burns thought of as "the Great Mutiny" died not with a bang but a whimper. The sale of beer was resumed in the enlisted men's mess, and a fresh start made on the art gallery. (The colonel declined, however, an eleven-by-fourteen inch color photograph of Major Houlihan, taken the day the shower-tent wall fell down and offered by Captains Pierce and McIntyre as the first work of art for display in the new art gallery.) And while the colonel continued the "temporary" abandonment of reveille and close-order drill, he also flatly forbade any further reference to Majors Burns and Houlihan as "Romeo and Juliet," "Beauty and the L'il Beastie," or anything else that suggested their relationship was somewhat unmilitary, not to mention unchaste.

The uneasy truce lasted until the next time Colonel Blake was ordered from the 4077th MASH on temporary duty and Major Burns again took command by virtue of his rank. Possessed of what Hawkeye referred to as a "weasel-like shrewdness," Major Burns did not, this time, attempt to enforce his notions of proper military behavior on the male officers, but rather restricted himself to harassing the enlisted men and the nurses.

In the case of the latter, Captains Pierce and McIntyre scheduled professional medical lectures (which had priority) whenever Major Burns' "order of the day" called for close-order drill, trench digging, or whatever. But this left the enlisted men, again, catching all the nonsense. Hawkeye and Trapper John were always able to frustrate Frank Burns' plans eventually, but it was usually after the fact. And before countermeasures could be put into play, the troops suffered.

Like seven or eight million others who have answered their draft boards' summonses only to find a slimy viper curled round the flagpole, Hawkeye and Trapper John vowed solemn retribution against their viper, such retribution to take place after they had been discharged.

Unlike the others, however, Hawkeye and Trapper John did not let this burning desire for sweet justice flicker out and die when they went home. It is true, of course, they didn't go through with their announced intention to roast ex-Major Burns, *à la* the Apache custom, upside down over a slow fire, nor did the opportunity present itself to tie Frank Burns' major extremities to four large horses and send the horses galloping off in four different directions.

They eked out their revenge in more subtle ways.

Each March 13, for example, Florists' Telegraph Delivery delivered to Dr. Burns' Hillandale, Ohio, residence one large potted passion flower, together with a card reading, "Thinking of You on Our Day."

March 13 was the anniversary of the day Hawkeye and Trapper John had, after slipping Major Burns a strong sedative in his tea, encased him to his neck in plaster of Paris; they took some pleasure in knowing that Mrs. Burns would not know this.

And through the year, as they thumbed through magazines, they carefully tore out, and filled out, in

Major Burns' name, all the postage-paid business-reply coupons, offering such things as lifetime subscriptions to the Bee-Keeper's Journal ("Send no money till February!") or a complete record library for only 99 cents down and $18.90 a month for the rest of one's life.

They had met, face to face, just once in all the years that had passed. Dr. Burns had left the practice of pediatric medicine for a specialty that was both inimical to pediatrics and paid better. He was the founder and president of the Burns Vasectomological Institute, where $250 ("Easy Terms Available") bought a fifteen-minute quasi-surgical procedure known in the trade as tube-snipping.

Even physicians engaged in such a noble enterprise as making irreversible contributions toward zero population growth needed rest, relaxation, and the company of their peers. Dr. Burns had gone to New Orleans, Louisiana, to attend the National Convention of the American College of Tonsil, Adenoid and Vas Deferens Surgeons (more popularly known as the TA & VD Society). By coincidence, Dr. Pierce and Dr. McIntyre had happened to be in the Crescent City at the same time. The press of their duties, however, had been such that no opportunity had arisen to, as Dr. Pierce told Dr. McIntyre, "Give old Frank what he really deserves."*

What Doctors Pierce and McIntyre felt that Dr. Burns really deserved cannot be reported in a fine, morally uplifting volume such as this without resorting to the most shameless euphemisms. Suffice it to say that when the telephone in Dr. Pierce's office rang they had just completed phase one of project "Where Frank Walks."

Phase one had involved dealing with chemists who worked for the nation's largest herbicide manufacturers. They now had in their hands a product known

* The details of the visit of Doctors Pierce and McIntyre to New Orleans have been recorded for posterity, for those with an interest in the extra-ordinary, in a neatly glued-together volume entitled, *M*A*S*H Goes to New Orleans* (Pocket Books, New York).

as Dichlorobichloroalkamkydchlestrolal B13 (short title DCC-B13), .001 cc of which was absolutely guarranteed not only to instantly kill any grass it came in contact with, but also to so contaminate the surrounding soil, for a distance of eighteen inches, that grass would not grow there again for at least three years.

Dr. Burns, when he could spare the time from counting the money the Burns Vasemological Institute brought in, was a devoted golfer. And Hawkeye and Trapper John had recently learned that, after having been denied admission on twelve separate occasions, Dr. Burns had finally been admitted to membership in the Hillandale Country Club.

So, when the telephone rang, Dr. Pierce and Dr. McIntyre were lovingly injecting one syringe-full after another of Dichlorobichloroalkamkydchlestrolal B-13 into the soles of a brand-new pair of golf shoes. Miss Miller was writing—in a hand obviously female and full of loops, whirls, and little circles instead of periods and dots—a little letter to accompany the shoes, telling Dr. Burns they were the little gift of someone who admired him from afar but was too shy to tell him so to his face.

With a little bit of luck, Frank Burns' first round of golf on the Hillandale links would be something that would be remembered for years.

Chapter Three

"If you'll forgive my saying so, Doctors," Student Nurse Barbara Ann Miller said, "this is really rotten!" She giggled with delight.

"I should hope so," Dr. Pierce replied, "considering what this Dichlorobichloroalkamkydchlestrolal cost us."

"Fish-eye Frank Burns, M.D., must really be a terrible man!" Miss Miller said.

"You know that professional ethics forbid me to comment adversely on either the professional skill or moral character of a fellow healer," Dr. Pierce said, "but you said it, sweetie!"

This was when the telephone rang. Miss Miller grabbed it on the first ring.

"Dr. Pierce's office," she said. "Dr. Pierce is in conference and cannot be disturbed unless in case of medical emergency."

She blushed at the reply and extended the phone to Hawkeye.

"Who is it?" he asked.

"I don't know," she confessed.

"Did you tell him that I'm not talking unless there's a medical emergency?"

"Yes, sir," she said. "And he said that unless you come on the line, there *will* be a medical emergency."

Curiosity got the better of Dr. Pierce and he reached for the phone. "Did he say what kind of an emergency?" he asked, covering the phone with his hand.

Barbara Ann Miller nodded her head and blushed.

"Well?"

"He said unless you got on the phone in two seconds he personally would bust your gluteus maximus,* Doctor."

"Who the hell is this?" Dr. Pierce said into the phone. "And who the hell do you think you are, interrupting my conference?"

The other three looked at him rather fondly as he said this. He was often at his best when telling someone off. What happened next, however, surprised and even shocked the others in the room.

"Yes, sir!" Dr. Pierce said. "This is me, sir. I hope you'll forgive me for any delay, sir. If I had only known you would be good enough to call."

For a moment Trapper John thought that Hawkeye was working up to some masterful sarcastic putdown of the caller, but then he recognized, from the look of pain in his friend's eyes, that Hawkeye was really sorry about something. Curiosity got the better of *him*, too, and he reached up and punched the button that placed both ends of the call on loudspeakers. He did this in time to amplify the caller's next comment.

"And what about that bum McIntyre? Is he sober enough to talk?"

Nurse Flanagan's mouth, and that of Miss Miller, dropped open in shock.

"Yes, sir," Trapper John said, coming to attention. "Quite sober, sir. And how are you, Doctor?"

"As well, to coin a phrase," the gruff and hearty voice replied, "as can be expected under the circumstances, the circumstances being that I celebrated my sixtieth birthday last Thursday."

"Happy Birthday, Doctor!" Pierce and McIntyre said in duet.

---

* The gluteus maximus are muscles *inside* what is commonly known as the rump. Dr. Grogarty knew this, as most physicians do, and consequently this is not exactly what he said he was going to bust if Hawkeye did not answer the phone.

"I got your presents," the caller said. "Considering all the money you two blots on the Hippocratic escutcheon are stealing from your patients, it seems to me that you could have done better than two lousy cases of twelve-year-old Scotch."

"It's all we could get here, sir," Hawkeye said. "We'll do better next time."

"Next week," Trapper John corrected.

"Tomorrow!" Hawkeye said.

"How can we be of service, Doctor?" Trapper John asked.

Both Dr. Pierce and Dr. McIntyre had spent (at different times) several years as surgical residents at the Grogarty Clinic. Dr. Grogarty's classroom and operating-ampitheater instruction had been of such high quality that both Hawkeye and Trapper John felt they owed a large part of whatever skill they had to him.

"I need an outside opinion," Dr. Grogarty said.

"From *us,* sir?" Hawkeye asked, visibly surprised.

"You mean you actually want an opinion from one of *us?*" Trapper John asked.

"This patient's pretty important to me," Dr. Grogarty said. "I've already got half a dozen opinions, each one from a surgeon who makes you guys look like first-year residents, but I figured, what the hell, why not ask. Wisdom from the mouth of babes, so to speak."

"Anything we can do, sir," Hawkeye said. "We're honored that you would ask."

"Don't let it go to your head," Dr. Grogarty said. "I've had my girl send some x-rays and an EKG and some other stuff over the line. Are you sober enough to look at it, or should I call back in the morning?"

"We'll look at it right now, sir," Hawkeye said. Trapper John was already on his way out the door toward the data room.

The diagnosis did not take long, and the prognosis was not favorable.

"I'm afraid your patient, in my judgement," Hawkeye said, very formally, "is in trouble."

"What I'm trying to find out, Hawkeye," Dr. Grogarty said, "is how bad you think that trouble is?"

"There's no question in my mind about the cancerous lung. A two to three pack a day smoker, I'd say. For at least twenty years."

"You think the lungs are too far gone?"

"No, I could jerk the right and take out about half the left," Hawkeye said. "If I could operate. But not with that heart. That heart's about to let go. The trauma of surgery . . ." He left the rest unsaid.

"Trapper John?" Dr. Grogarty asked.

"I concur," Trapper John said formally. "I don't think he'd last three minutes on the table."

"Well, think of some gentle way to break the news to him," Dr. Grogarty said.

"Sir?"

"He's on his way to see you," Dr. Grogarty said. "Flying by private plane, and accompanied by his personal physician . . . who happens to be his son."

"I don't quite understand, sir," Hawkeye said.

"It's very simple, Hawkeye," Dr. Grogarty said. "I don't have the guts to tell a guy I've known all my life, who has just found out that he's wasted the last twenty-five years of his life, what his life expectancy is. And I think he'd rather get it from total strangers."

"Jesus Christ!" Hawkeye said.

"His name is Charley Whiley," Dr. Grogarty said. "And don't worry about professional courtesy about your bill because of his son. He's loaded."

"Thanks a lot," Hawkeye said.

"You're welcome," Dr. Grogarty said. "I never thought I'd say this to you two, but I owe you one."

And with that, the telephone went dead.

Hawkeye pushed the button and shut the telephone off. Esther Flanagan, R.N., a lady of generous proportions, a formidable appearance, and very gentle eyes, went to the martini mixer and from it poured two large fresh martinis.

She gave one each to Hawkeye and Trapper John,

and then picked up the telephone and dialed a number.

"Esther Flanagan calling for Dr. Pierce. We'll need a private room for a Mr. Whiley. And call down to the Spruce Harbor Home-Away-From-Home Motel and Barbecue and reserve a room . . . away from the pool and bar . . . for a Dr. Whiley."

"Thanks," Hawkeye said.

"I was about to say 'my pleasure,' " Esther Flanagan said. "What did the x-rays show?"

"An embolism," Hawkeye said. "One that could let go any minute."

"Like now, when he's flying here in his own airplane?"

"Like now, when he's flying here in his own airplane," Trapper John said. "Let's hope that his son is one of those flying doctors you hear about."

"Whatever was Dr. Grogarty thinking of? Wasn't that sort of playing God?" she asked.

"I think it falls into the category of putting it in God's hands," Hawkeye said. "I just figured out who this guy is."

"Who is he?" Trapper John said.

"There is—or was—a picture of him on Grogarty's office wall. Shows the two of them in China during World War II. He was one of those dashing young men in the silk scarves and leather jackets . . . Flying Tigers."

"I remember the picture," Trapper John said.

"Maybe Grogarty figures the way he'd like to go is playing birdman," Hawkeye said. "Off we go—and keep going—into the wild blue yonder!"

"He may have a point," Trapper John said. "I've always thought I'd like to go, at ninety-eight or so, by shooting at the hands of a jealous-with-reason husband."

"There's no hope at all, Hawkeye?" Student Nurse Miller asked.

"There is *always* hope," Hawkeye replied. "Or that, at least, is the popular folklore."

"I guess this all seems pretty silly, doesn't it?"

Barbara Ann Miller said, gesturing at the golf shoes on the desk.

"How wrong you are, my little chickadee," Hawkeye said. "At moments like these, if it weren't for the prospect of wreaking oh-so-sweet revenge on Frank Burns, I would go quite bananas. Where were we?"

"I was just about to finish the letter. How should I sign it?"

"Let me think," Hawkeye said. "How about 'tenderly'?"

"How about 'shyly'?"

"How about," Esther Flanagan said, " 'with shy and tender passion'?"

"You've missed your calling, Flanagan," Hawkeye said. " 'With shy and tender passion' it is."

Barbara Ann Miller wrote the words on the paper with some difficulty. Her eyes were rather watery.

At this very moment, at the Burns Vasectomological Clinic of Hillandale, Ohio, Francis Burns, M.D., was also in touch with San Francisco, California, also known as "The City by the Bay," through the facilities of Ma Bell.*

By bending the truth just a little (he had informed the vice-president for charitable affairs of the Mark Hopkins Hotel that the organization with which he was connected provided care, free of charge, to impoverished orphans, and that his purpose in traveling to San Francisco was to participate in a medical conference), he had arranged for rooms at a great discount.**

---

* The attentive reader will recall that the time is after six. Since Ma Bell, out of the bottomless goodness of its corporate heart, reduces rates after that hour, it was Dr. Burns' custom to make all of his long-distance calls after six. He had never forgotten the profound wisdom, courtesy of Benjamin Franklin, that he had picked up in the second grade—"A penny saved is a penny earned." Unfortunately, each time he called it to mind he was reminded, very painfully, of a chap named Benjamin Franklin Pierce.

** There was a *germ* of truth in what he said and how he said it. He had innocently dropped the descriptive word "vasemological" from the name of his institution, and it was perfectly true that the "Burns Institute" would offer its services, free of charge, to any impoverished orphan who

"God bless you, sir!" Frank Burns now said to the vice-president for charitable affairs. "I'm sure our little ones, when they are physically able, will remember you in their prayers!"

Then he hung up and telephoned Mrs. Burns, to whom he referred—depending on the circumstances —as either "Sweetie-Baby" or "the little woman."

"Well," he said, with just a touch of pride in his somewhat nasal voice, "we're fixed up at the Mark Hopkins. All you have to do now is arrange for your mother to care for the kids while we're gone. You get on the telephone and ask her to come. And don't forget to stress the fact that travel by bus is really better than flying for someone her age. It's only thirty-six hours on a nonstop bus from her house to ours."

Frank Burns, as incredible as it might sound and as difficult as it might be to accept, actually had a devious purpose in going to San Francisco. He had, several months before, while unwrapping some medical equipment he had purchased at a very good price from a dealer in military surplus, come across something in a newspaper (the World War II vintage scalpels and forceps, which were a little rusty but would clean up nicely, had been wrapped in old newspapers) that had set his heart aflutter.

In the old newspaper there had been a photograph of a statuesque lady, dressed in a long gown and a cape, her hands raised in a gesture of blessing. The caption with the picture had confirmed what Frank Burns had thought, with a quickening of his heart, the moment he saw the lady's mammiform protuberances straining against the gown. It *was* his beloved Margaret!

"GOD IS LOVE IN ALL FORMS CHRISTIAN CHURCH PRELATE RETURNS HOME TO SAN FRANCISCO," a line

---

asked for them. The hook here was that, because of the nature of vasemological procedures, it was illegal to perform them upon minors, and Dr. Burns would never knowingly break the law. And he was, indeed, going to confer on medical matters while in San Francisco. He had every intention of conferring with Mrs. Burns, of asking her right out if the aspirin he had prescribed for her headache a week before had been effective in reducing her distress.

over the picture had read, and beneath the photograph there had been this caption:

SAN FRANCISCO, CALIF. Shown as she blessed the welcoming crowd that surrounded her arriving aircraft this afternoon at San Francisco International Airport is Rev. Mother Emeritus Margaret H. W. Wilson, of the God Is Love In All Forms Christian Church, Inc. The Reverend Mother Wilson and several members of her staff returned home to San Francisco today. The GILIAFCC, Inc., was founded here by the Reverend Mother's late husband, the Blessed Reverend Buck Wilson.

She was greeted at the airport by San Francisco Police Commissioner Boulder J. Ohio, and immediately went by motorcade to the GILIAFCC, Inc. . . .

At that point, the story had ended. Some callous and unthinking person had ripped the newspaper, and although he'd searched diligently through all the rusty scalpels and forceps, Frank Burns had not been able to find the rest of it.

He came to realize, however, that what he had was enough. Margaret, his beloved Margaret, his bosom pal of his war years, his fellow field-grade officer and gentleperson, whom he had seen but once (and then all too briefly) since the war, was not only in San Francisco, but also a widow.

While he was, of course, profoundly sorry that whatshisname had kicked the bucket, he could not help but consider that if she was a widow, that meant there was no need to worry about a jealous husband.

Furthermore, Frank Burns knew (from two experiences) that he was *very* good when it came to consoling widows, and he'd always felt that he could have gotten even better at it had it not been for buttinsky neighbors and relatives who for some reason never seemed to be willing to leave him alone with the bereaved.

The only thing that stood between him and the resumption of what he fondly remembered as a *splendid* relationship with Margaret was getting to San Francisco. He dwelt on the mental image of what would happen when she saw him again.

"Margaret!" he would say.

"Frank," Margaret would say.

"Margaret," he would repeat.

"Frank!" she would say again. And then she would rush into his arms.

And this time, of course, there would be no Benjamin Franklin Pierce or John F. X. McIntyre around to remind Margaret about Sweetie-Baby and the kids.

The only problem, then, was getting to San Francisco —soon, and alone. This proved more difficult than he expected. Sweetie-Baby pointed out that in the long years of her marriage she had been away with him only three times. On their honeymoon, all the way to Chillicothe; to Columbus, when he'd left for the Army; and, just two years ago, to New Orleans. None of these journeys had really been pleasant, she pointed out to him. He certainly (she said) could not forget what had happened on their honeymoon, and even if what he said about that happening to a lot of newlyweds was true, he did have to agree with her (she said), that it hadn't been much fun.

And when she'd gone to Columbus with him, to see him off to the Army, that hadn't been much fun for her either. He had cried the night through in the Econo-Cheap Motel. And in New Orleans, he had gotten sick.*

"So I made up my mind, Francis," Sweetie-Baby said, "after talking it over with mama, of course, that the next time you leave town, I'm going with you."

---

* In New Orleans, he had modestly informed a newspaper reporter that he had been General McArthur's personal physician while in the Far East—an innocent little exaggeration. He had fallen sick immediately upon learning that Doctors Pierce and McIntyre were also in New Orleans; they had not only been in the Far East with him, but also were about to talk to the same reporter. The details are available, told without fear or favor, and in a style described as "certainly odd" in *M*A*S*H Goes to New Orleans* (Pocket Books, New York).

Nothing he said or did could make her change her mind. Finally, in desperation, he decided he would have to take her along and worry about how to get rid of her once he was in San Francisco. He could, he thought, send her out to ride the cable cars—they were cheap enough—while he pleaded a sick headache. Anyway, he would think of *something*. Nothing could be permitted to come between Margaret and him.

When he hung up on Sweetie-Baby, he went to the mirror and examined himself with quiet pride. What woman could ask for more?

And far across the wide Atlantic in Paris, France, at just about this same time, something else was happening that would in a short time also have an effect on San Francisco, California.

The balalaika player at the Casanova, a well-known, long-established night club (or *boîte de nuit,* which translates literally as "box of night" for those interested in such things) on Rue Pierre Charron, was smashed out of his mind.

What had brought him to this state of senselessness was not known, nor indeed will it ever be known. All that is remembered of the incident is that as the "witching hour" approached * and the assistant undermanager went to summon him from his room in order to tune up before making an appearance, he found the balalaika player, previously a responsible, respectable, near teetotaler, sitting on the window ledge of his dressing room clutching a bottle of brandy to his chest and singing bawdy songs to an appreciative audience of hookers who stood below on the sidewalk.

The clientele of the Casanova had come, over the years, to expect that their musical entertainment would consist of soft, moody, and above all romantic numbers, suitable background for the gentle burbling

* In Paris, France, the "witching hour," or midnight, means, among other things, that musicians required to ply their trade go on overtime, or time- and-a-half. This is why the Casanova has eight fiddlers playing from eight to midnight, and one balalaika player from midnight on.

noise champagne makes when being poured into fine crystal glasses. Ladies and gentlemen came to the Casanova, frankly, with romance on their minds. Neither seductors nor seductees would, the assistant undermanager instantly realized, be at all happy with a balalaika player who was not only unable to stand up without assistance but who was bellowing, at the top of his lungs, in rather dreadful English, all the verses of "Roll Me Over, Yankee Soldier," which he had learned in the closing days of World War II (when he had accompanied a unit of the Second Armored Division in its dash across France).

He brought the problem to the attention of his immediate superior, the undermanager himself, who personally left his post to see for himself, and promptly had hysterics. The assistant undermanager took it upon himself to inform the manager himself.

"Pierre," the manager said, "the honor of the Casanova is at stake! In its hour of crisis, I call upon you to shoulder the responsibility!"

"Just tell me what I can do," Pierre replied.

"Go get me a balalaika player, you idiot! And immediately!"

"Yes, sir!"

"And hurry! Every minute I have to keep the fiddle players past midnight, they're getting time-and-a-half!"

One cannot, of course, even in Paris, France, call up the friendly musicians local at midnight and ask them to send a balalaika player right over. For one thing, the musicians union is closed at that hour, and for another, balalaika players in Paris are about as common as they are in, say, Hillandale, Ohio.

The assistant undermanager, faced with this problem, did what any Parisian would do under the circumstances. First he had a strong cognac, and then he sought the assistance of a taxi driver.

The cab driver shrugged his shoulders helplessly.

"I know of no at-liberty balalaika players," he said finally. "Perhaps m'sieu would settle for a trumpet player? Or perhaps a guitar player?"

A trumpet player was obviously out of the question,

but there were possibilities in a guitar player. If nothing else, a guitar player, starting fresh, would not be on time-and-a-half for overtime.

"Take me to the guitar player," the assistant undermanager cried, leaping into the taxi.

They crossed the Seine onto what is known as the Left Bank, and, after negotiating a number of narrow, picturesque streets, stopped before an establishment from which came the sounds of Spanish flamenco music.

For the purpose of the Casanova, Spanish flamenco music was about as useful as a trumpet player playing the overture to *William Tell* or the opening bars of the triumphal march from *Aïda*—that is to say, it was not the sort of music in which either seductor or seductee would really be much interested—but, with no other alternative, the assistant undermanager went into the establishment, which was identified by a neon sign as El Gaucho.

Immediately inside the door he came across a young, black-haired man who had a guitar with him and was drinking from a glass of water.

"I seek a musician," the assistant undermanager said to him.

"I regret, sir, inasmuch as I am quite without funds and desperately need employment, that I am probably not your man. I am here to listen to these flamenco guitarists in the hope that I can learn that form of music and one day find a job."

"You talk funny, you know that?" the assistant undermanager said.

"I regret, sir, that while my French is more or less fluent, it is not the French of the common man. I learned my French in a monastery, where the good brothers were Russian exiles, not Frenchmen."

"Russian? You're putting me on!"

"No, sir. I was educated at the monastery of St. Igor in my native San Sebastian."

"You're kidding!"

"No, sir. Unfortunately, the music they taught me was the music of Russia, and I find to my distress that this is not a very saleable commodity in Paris, France."

"I don't suppose you can play the balalaika?"

"Oh, yes," the young man said. "But I do not despair. I am presently conducting negotiations with an interior decorator. If good fortune smiles on me, he will exchange a Spanish guitar for my poor old balalaika." He held up the case to show the assistant undermanager his instrument. From its shape, the assistant undermanager of the Casanova recognized that it was a balalaika case (the bottom of a balalaika is generally round, rather than flat, as a guitar's is).

Within ten seconds, the young man and his balalaika were out of the El Gaucho and inside the taxicab.

En route to the Casanova, the assistant undermanager learned some of the young man's background. He had been sent to Paris to attend the Sorbonne, but there had been a revolution in San Sebastian, and, as a result of that revolution, his father had been jailed, and there was no money for his education.

He had given up hope of going to the Sorbonne, and all he hoped for now was to be able to find a job that would permit him to eat. He had not eaten in three days, he said.

At the Casanova, he was hurriedly dressed in a Russian peasant costume, hurriedly fed a ham sandwich, and literally pushed out onto the floor.

To the profound relief of the manager (who immediately kissed the assistant undermanager on both cheeks and then ordered him to throw "the other bum" out), the young man was just what they were looking for. He immediately began to play a continuous medley of Russian songs that caused the patrons to cling affectionately to each other and not pay much attention to how much champagne was left in the champagne bottles when the waiters removed them and brought fresh ones.

After seeing how well he had been received by his patrons, after hearing his sad tale of his impoverished friendless condition, and after determining that he was alone in an alien country, the manager immediately prepared a contract that guaranteed the young balalaika player a place to sleep, his choice of left-overs from customers' dinners, and a salary in francs that came to about $23.50 per week in dollars. In return he agreed to play for six hours a night, seven nights a week, starting at midnight.

Thus Pancho Hermanez came to the Casanova and began his new life.

Chapter Four

At about the time that Dr. Grogarty placed his call to Dr. Pierce, a dozen singers, dressed in the costumes of the eighteenth century, faced the audience of the Bolshoi Theatre of Grand Opera and Ballet in Moscow, took deep breaths, and belted out together, or *ensemble,* as they say in grand opera, the final lines of the current production, "This is the evil-doer's end—sinners finally meet their just reward and always will."

As the conductor's baton guided the Moscow Philharmonic Orchestra through the final bars of Wolfgang Amadeus Mozart's *Don Giovanni,* the curtain descended. There was a moment's silence as the music died, and the curtain's rustling was the only sound to be heard in the enormous theater. And then the applause began, accompanied by screams and moans of ecstasy. Someone cried out a name: "Boris!" This was picked up immediately by others, until the fine crystal chandeliers and the heavy red curtain itself shook with the vibrations of the name. *"Boris! Boris! Boris! Boris!"*

Down each aisle, dressed in their very best parade uniforms, sixty officers of the Guards Regiment came at a trot to form a semicircle before the orchestra pit. Once they were in place, lines of ushers started down the aisle; each usher bore an enormous basket of cut flowers.

The huge curtain parted just enough to permit one

man to step before the footlights. Dressed in the costume in which he had just sung the title role, Boris Alexandrovich Korsky-Rimsakov bounded gracefully onto the stage and up to the footlights, his arms raised high in acknowledgement of the audience's appreciation.

He stood six feet five inches tall. The full, jet-black beard that accented his dark Slavic eyes was his own. As he raised his arms again and again, his forty-six-inch chest strained against his lace shirt.

One by one the baskets of cut flowers were laid at his feet as he continued to acknowledge the tumultuous, almost hysterical applause of the audience. From time to time, his eyes dropped to the front rows of the theater, where the sixty officers, chosen for their size, barely managed to restrain three dozen women of all sizes and shapes (but tending toward the middle-aged and well-nourished) who, screaming his name, were attempting to force their way onto the stage.

Finally, he raised his voice. "My children!" he said, his basso profundo nearly overwhelmed by the waves of applause. He repeated the phrase again, this time calling forth what had often been described as his "incredible vocal power."

He raised his hands once again, very high over his head, and then lowered them, palms downward. The noise, the tumult, died as he did so. By the time his hands reached the level of his waist, the enormous theater was silent—except for the sobbing of some women who had been forced to conclude they could not force their way past the Guards Regiment officers.

"My children," he said softly. His voice nevertheless filled the room. "I, Boris Alexandrovich Korsky-Rimsakov, thank you for coming to hear me sing."

This occasioned another burst of applause from the left. Boris frowned, raised his left hand, and let it fall again. Silence returned.

"And now I must leave you," Boris continued. "Forget me not!"

The applause swelled up again, this time mingled

with cries of "Don't leave us! Stay forever!" and other sentiments of this nature.

He bowed deeply and turned to the curtain to make his departure. A microphone on a long cable descended from the proscenium arch in time to pick up and transmit throughout the theater the singer's inquiry, in English, "Now, where the hell is the goddamn flap?"

From stage right, a portly gentleman attired in the dress uniform of a commissar of the Soviet Union marched onstage, trailed by sixteen members of his official entourage, also in their dress uniforms.

"Maestro," this Soviet luminary cried, "you are magnificent!"

"Yes, I know," Boris replied, in fluent Russian. "How the hell do I get out of here?"

"I come as an official delegate of the Supreme Soviet," the official said.

"Good for you," the singer replied, tugging at the curtain and looking for the flap.

"It is my great honor, Boris Alexandrovich Korsky-Rimsakov," the official replied, "to inform you that you have been awarded the medal of a Hero of the Soviet Arts." He turned over his shoulder and one of his aides handed him a small box, from which he took a star knotted to a red ribbon.

"Maestro," he said, "dear Boris Alexandrovich . . ."

"Are you going to show me how to get out of here or not?" Boris demanded.

"We want to give you your medal!"

"I already have one," Boris said. "The damned things aren't even gold, just polished brass. I loathe polished brass. The U.S. Army has a polished brass fetish."

". . . And to once again offer you, dear Boris Alexandrovich, on behalf of the Supreme Soviet, a warm welcome plus status as a Premiere Artist of the Russian People, if you will only stay here in the home of your ancestors."

"I've been over all this before," Boris replied impatiently. "The only reason I come here once a year is to take a look at Uncle Sergei's theater for him."

"Uncle Sergei?"

"The Grand Duke Sergei Korsky-Rimsakov," Boris replied. "He owns this theater."

"An artist such as yourself," the commissar of the Soviet Union said, flushing, "should not trouble his genius with politics."

"Politics? Politics? Who's talking about politics? I'm talking about money. Uncle Sergei hasn't gotten a dime out of this place since 1917. *Money's* what I'm talking about."

"This is the People's Opera House!"

"The hell it is," Boris said. "It's my Uncle Sergei's. He bought it from the czar, and I've got the bill of sale to prove it."

"About the medal," the commissar of the Soviet Union said.

"If I take the damned thing, will you show me how to get off the stage?"

"Of course, dear Boris Alexandrovich," the commissar said.

"O.K., then," Boris replied. "But make it quick."

He turned to face the commissar, who stood on his tiptoes and pinned the medal to Boris' massive chest.

"Congratulations, Boris Alexandrovich Korsky-Rimsakov, Soviet Hero of the Arts!" the commissar said.

"If this gets back to my chapter of the John Birch Society," Boris said, "I'll get thrown out on my ass, that's what'll happen."

"The President of the Supreme Soviet hopes that your schedule will permit you to join him, the other commissars, and their wives for a little reception," the commissar said.

"Like hell," Boris said. "I've been here three days, and I haven't had a decent meal or a decent drink the whole time. While I am prepared to make nearly any sacrifice for my art, I stop short of dying of starvation and thirst. It's off to the airport for me."

Finally, without assistance from the commissar, he found where the curtain halves overlapped, spread them apart, and disappeared backstage.

Thirty minutes later, a Zis limousine rolled up beside an ungainly droop-nosed jet aircraft at Moscow International Airport. The aircraft bore the legend AIR HUSSID on the fuselage and the Royal Hussidic coat of arms on the tail.*

Boris erupted from the back seat of the car and bounded up the stairs into the plane. A white-jacketed steward took his coat from him and then followed him into the royal cabin. As Boris settled himself into a goatskin upholstered chair, the steward slid a footrest under his feet.

"May I bring you something, Maestro?" he asked.

"A little snack," the singer replied. "Couple of bottles of bubbly, a steak, a couple of baked potatoes, and maybe a couple of dozen oysters to get started."

"Immediately, Maestro," the steward said.

"And tell his nibs to get this show on the road," Boris said. "Where is he, anyway? Why wasn't he waiting for me backstage?"

His Royal Highness Prince Hassan ad Kayam had, several years before, attached himself to the world's greatest opera singer—that is, Boris. It wasn't that His Royal Highness particularly liked grand opera, but rather that he had noticed that Boris' female discards were of greater variety and higher quality than he had been able to get on the open market, despite the facts that it was generally known that his income ran to some $35,000 per day and that he had no objection to paying for quality.

Boris had come to tolerate, even accept, His Royal Highness' faithful presence. There was the airplane, for one thing, which beat standing in line to be insulted by airline ticket personnel, and Hassan considered it

---

* Of the eight Le Discorde supersonic jet transports sold so far, two each have been sold to the Air France and British Airways, and four to Air Hussid, which is owned by the sheikh of Hussid. Only the sheikh, whose petroleum income is estimated at $1.2 million per day, is in a position to absorb the $1.35 per-mile-per-seat expense of operating the *pièce de résistance* of Anglo-French aviation technology. The heir apparent to the throne of Hussid, His Royal Highness Sheikh Hassan ad Kayam, Boris' buddy, had been given the aircraft Boris boarded in Moscow to facilitate his diplomatic duties.

a privilege to be accorded the honor of picking up all Boris' bills, thus sparing Boris to devote his full attention to his art. (The art to which His Royal Highness made reference had nothing to do with grand opera.)

"His Royal Highness, Maestro," the steward said, "is not on board."

"Well, find him, and tell him to get his ass on board," Boris replied. "I don't like to be kept waiting. Besides, he's wasting his time. With the exception of the corps de ballet, none of the game around here is worthy of the chase. Unless you happen to be a fat freak."

"Prince Hassan, Maestro," the steward said, as he skillfully popped the cork of a jeroboam of Piper Heidsieck '48, "is in San Francisco."

"What is he doing in San Francisco? *I* didn't give him permission to go to San Francisco."

"He said to tell you that he would be sure to pay his respects to your sister, Maestro."

"He'd damned well better," Boris said. "She was, after all, good enough to invite him to her wedding." He drained a twelve-ounce crystal chalice of the Piper Heidsieck '48 and held it out to be refilled. "Esmerelda and the baroness are aboard, I take it?" he asked. "I will see them now."

He referred to Esmerelda Hoffenburg, the ballerina, and the Baroness d'Iberville, who were members of what was known as the *cercle intime,* those privileged to spend a good deal of time close—in the case of the baroness and Esmerelda, *very* close—to the man widely proclaimed as the world's greatest opera singer.

"No, Maestro," the steward said nervously. "The baroness and Esmerelda are with His Royal Highness in San Francisco."

"You're telling me that I've been deserted in my hour of need? That I am alone on this airplane? What the hell are the baroness and Esmerelda doing in San Francisco?"

"It would seem, Maestro, that His Royal Highness the Sheikh of Abzug wished to go to San Francisco."

64

"Abdullah, too? What the hell is going on in San Francisco that I don't know about?"

"His Royal Highness, you will recall, Maestro, was disconsolate when you told him he couldn't accompany you to Moscow."

"You know what happened the last time!" Boris said. "He tried to buy Lenin's tomb. He said he needed a little man with a beard for *his* wax museum. All they had to say was no, for God's sake, but you know these Bolsheviks, always overreacting. I told him there was nothing shameful in being declared *persona non grata* in Moscow. My own Uncle Sergei—and he's a grand duke—is *persona non grata.*"

"Yes, yes, Maestro. In any event, when His Royal Highness couldn't go with you, he grew lonely. So he telephoned Mr. J. Robespierre O'Reilly, and Mr. O'Reilly apparently asked His Royal Highness* to come and visit and play a little poker."

"So what's that got to do with Hassan and the girls?"

"Well, Maestro, you know that sometimes when His Royal Highness the Sheikh of Abzug gets off by himself, he is, what shall I say, misunderstood?"

"And?"

"Since he is also more or less *persona non grata* in Moscow, Prince Hassan thought it might be a good idea to go after His Royal Highness."

"Abdullah's not going to get into trouble in San Francisco," Boris announced. "Radar O'Reilly is a real square."

"And since Prince Hassan was going, Maestro, the ladies thought they might as well go along, too."

"What you're telling me, then, is that I really have been left alone on this dangerous airplane."

"Well, there's the pilot, Maestro, and the copilot. And the flight engineer. And the chef. And the wine steward. And myself. And His Royal Highness has placed the airplane at your complete disposal," the

---

* Mr. O'Reilly and His Royal Highness the Sheikh of Abzug became friends when the latter was more or less an uninvited guest at the former's wedding. The full details have been made public in *M*A*S*H Goes to Las Vegas* (Pocket Books, New York), popularly priced at a low, low buck and a half.

steward said. "On our arrival in Paris, His Royal Highness' limousine and His Royal Highness' bodyguards will of course be waiting for you, Maestro."

"You're admitting it, then," Boris said. "I *have* been deserted by that sawed-off camel jockey."

The conversation was cut off at that moment. The pilot had started the engines. When Le Discorde engines started, the resulting noise and vibration was such that even the pilot and copilot had to communicate with each other by means of handheld blackboards. In the passenger compartment the vibration made even that impossible.

It was only after the aircraft had taken off and reached cruising altitude that the noise level dropped to a point where conversation was again possible. By that time, the steward, who had previous experience dealing with the maestro, had had the foresight to absent himself from the royal cabin.

Boris was thus forced to console himself with what few creature comforts he could find at hand. After putting away the little snack, he opened a second jeroboam of Piper Heidsieck '48, put a tape recording of himself on the tape player, and then pushed a series of buttons that first caused a motion picture screen to appear on the forward cabin wall, and then a motion picture projector to start rolling. Singing along with himself, he devoted the rest of the trip to what he thought of as scientific research, his contribution to the betterment of mankind.

Specifically, he examined, with a professional, expert eye, some 16-mm color films sent to him 'for comment by Theosophilus Mullins Yancey, M.D. (founder and chief of staff of the T. Mullins Yancey Foundation of Manhattan, Kansas). From time to time, Boris made little entries in a notebook.

Dr. Yancey was a personal friend of the singer. They had met several years before, shortly after Dr. Yancey had published his famous treatise on exercise.*

* *Sexual Intercourse As Exercise* by T. Mullins Yancey, M.D., Ph.D., D.D., D.V.M. (1048 pp., illustrated, $9.95), The Yancey Foundation Press, Manhattan, Kansas.

In that now famous work, Dr. Yancey expounded the theory that one particular form of exercise was far superior in every way (especially insofar as it toned up the muscles and forced blood to the brain, thereby facilitating more profound thought) to such things as jogging, pushups, swimming, and so on.

Boris Alexandrovich Korsky-Rimsakov had recognized the book for the work of pure genius that it was as soon as he'd read it, and he'd written to Dr. Yancey to offer his congratulations. He had mentioned that he'd independently reached the same conclusions, and, in case the doctor might find his data of value in his work, had included several examples of how something he now correctly recognized as healthy exercise had improved his art.

Dr. Yancey had at first been rather sceptical of the stories, but his curiosity had been piqued to the point where he'd made discreet inquiries. A friend in the Department of State had told him it was absolutely true that Boris Alexandrovich Korsky-Rimsakov, during one of his annual visits to the U.S.S.R., had indeed "accommodated" the entire (female) corps de ballet of the Bolshoi—at least, those members of it over the age of sixteen. It was generally (if privately) admitted in diplomatic circles that it had been this accomplishment that had resulted in his being designated a Hero of the Soviet Arts. The official reason had been his performance in the title role of *Boris Godunov,* which had taken place the next day— knowledgeable opera buffs held the opinion that Boris' Boris had been better than Chaliapin's had ever been.

Over the years, both a professional relationship and a personal friendship had developed between the two men, and whenever Dr. Yancey's staff came up with some interesting film, an extra copy was run off to be sent to the singer for his professional evaluation.

The films Boris watched as the Le Discorde raced through the heavens toward Paris had been made, with the participants' permission,* during what is known in

---

* As Dr. T. Mullins Yancey was wont to confess, among his professional peers, "You wouldn't believe the weirdos we get out here."

some quarters as "physical congress." The participants were those who had (generally after reading *Playboy, Playgirl, Penthouse,* and other periodicals of this type) come to believe they were not getting out of their marriages (or dalliances) what others were. In a natural desire to get what nature intended them to have, they came, in droves, to Manhattan, Kansas, where, under the most professional circumstances, of course, they had at it before the foundation's cameras.

Once the film had been processed, it was run off before a special team of Yancey Foundation specialists —a gynecologist, a psychologist, and a contortionist. These experts then prepared a report suggesting how things could be improved. When there were unusual problems, Dr. Yancey always sent the film to Boris for his expert assessment. Other films were sent simply on the chance that Boris might be interested in them.

Three hours later, just before midnight, the Le Discorde swooped out of the sky like a drunken vulture and touched down at Paris' Orly International airfield. Although the strictest secrecy regarding Boris' travel schedule had been enforced, the word had somehow leaked out, and more than two hundred females were gathered at the field when the plane landed.

The Orly Field riot squad had, of course, been placed on standby for Boris' return. (Mr. Korsky-Rimsakov had been declared an Official Treasure of the French Republic some years before. This was both a tribute to his voice and to his ability to pack in customers at the Paris Opera. Whenever Boris Alexandrovich Korsky-Rimsakov sang at the opera, it was termed a "Performance Magnifique" and a 100-percent surcharge was imposed.)

A platoon of the riot squad had set up barriers and water hoses as a diversionary tactic, and the Korsky-Rimsakov fans had been fooled by it. They were still swarming around a remote corner of the huge field when the Le Discorde taxied right up to the main terminal building. With a precision that only long hours of practice had made possible, Boris' ground transportation swung up to the plane. First there was a Gendarmerie Nationale riot bus, from which forty stalwart, helmeted gendarmes leapt to form a corridor from the jet's steps. Next came a black Citröen limousine, bearing Corps Diplomatique license plates and flying the Royal Hussidic colors on the right front fender.

Six robed Arabs, each one bearing a silver-plated submachine gun, jumped out of the vehicle and took up positions inside the lines of gendarmes. Next a Cadillac limousine screeched to a halt. It, too, bore the Royal Hussidic coat of arms and the diplomatic license plates. Two more Arabs jumped out of this vehicle, one out of each side. The plane-side Arab held open the rear door of the Cadillac until the singer came running down the steps of the Le Discorde and jumped inside. The door was then slammed shut. The slammer and the other Arab then jumped into the front seat.

A radio signal was relayed and sirens and flashing lights on two waiting motorcycles burst into life. The limousine raced off behind them into the night.

There was a passenger in the back seat of the limousine waiting for Boris. With visible affection, he leaned over and kissed the singer wetly.

"God, I'm glad to see you, Prince," the singer said with obvious sincerity. "I missed you terribly in Moscow." The passenger kissed the singer again, rather fervently.

"Christ," the singer said. "Have you been rooting in garbage cans again, you mangy hound? Your breath would stop a clock!" He pushed the dog, a Scottish wolfhound, off the brocade upholstery onto the floor. The animal began to whine piteously.

"Stop that, for Christ's sake!" the singer said. "It will get you nowhere with me, and you know it!"

The dog whined even more piteously.

"Well, all right," the singer said. "You can get back on the seat, but for God's sake, breathe in the other direction!"

The dog climbed back on the seat, laid his head

on the singer's lap, and made a growl of contentment in his throat.

"It's you and me, Prince, alone and afraid in a world we never made," the singer said to the animal as he scratched his ears.

"To your apartment, Maestro?" the chauffeur's voice, over the intercom, asked.

"God, no!" the singer replied. "I couldn't bear to stare at those bare walls all by myself. Besides, it's only midnight. Take us to the Casanova."

"Your wish, Your Excellency," the chauffeur replied, "is my command."

"I know," Boris replied. "Step on it, Omar, will you? I ran out of bubbly somewhere over Poland."

Chapter Five

Boris had barely entered the Casanova, been shown to his table, and had his first jeroboam of bubbly opened when there was a disturbance at the entrance.

"What do you *mean, I* can't go in there?" an American voice said, in a basso very clearly as deep as Boris' basso, and in the inimitable (some say ludicrous) accents of those who have been educated at Harvard College and/or University. "My dear fellow, I am Matthew Q. Framingham, and I go wherever I wish!"

There was a pause, during which the assistant undermanager and the manager himself, while waving their hands in the peculiar manner of the French, explained that the alcove toward which this gentleman (who, at six-feet-four and 225 pounds, was sort of a seven-eighths scale replica of Boris—less, of course, the beard) was moving was occupied by Boris Alexandrovich Korsky-Rimsakov, and thus was off-limits to the general public.

"Let me assure you, sir," Mr. Framingham said, letting a bouncer who had sneaked up on him from the side have a short, but painful, thrust in the abdomen with the point of his umbrella, "that if it were not for the presence, for reasons which escape me, of Mr. Korsky-Rimsakov in this somewhat seedy and obviously disreputable establishment of yours, I would not be here myself. I *told* you who I was."

He was three-quarters of the way across the room now, close enough to alarm several members of His Royal Highness Prince Hassan's bodyguard. There was the sound of scimitars being drawn, and the oily click of submachine gun bolts being opened and closed.

71

Mr. Matthew Q. Framingham spotted Mr. Boris Alexandrovich Korsky-Rimsakov.

"Boris!" he said, somewhat peevishly. "Will you cause these terrible people to cease and desist?"

"Matthew!" Boris said in obvious delight, getting to his feet and tossing the jeroboam of champagne casually over his shoulder. "Little buddy! Goddamn, I'm glad to see you!"

Arms spread wide, Boris advanced on Matthew Q. Framingham.

"The emotion is reciprocal," Matthew said. He jabbed the manager, who was again getting closer to him than he liked, with the point of his umbrella, and then permitted himself to be embraced by Boris. Boris kissed him wetly, in the Russian manner, on each cheek, and then, wrapping him in a bear hug, lifted him off the ground.

"Goddamn, Matthew, I'm glad you're here!"

"For God's sake, Boris," Matthew Q. Framingham said, "put me down! Control your emotions!"

Boris did as he was ordered. He next draped his arm around Matthew's shoulder and led him to the table. Then he turned to the manager.

"Stop standing there with your mouth open and bring my little buddy something to drink," he ordered.

The Arab bodyguard resumed their positions, smiling uneasily.

"Where are the baroness and Esmerelda? And whatshisname, that Arab chap?" Matthew inquired. "The fat little fellow who flits around you like a bee pollinating?"

"In San Francisco," Boris said. "They left me alone and friendless. The perfidy of man never ceases to amaze me."

"How odd," Matthew said. He turned to glance over his shoulder and addressed the assistant undermanager. "I suppose it would be too much to hope that you have a decent cigar?"

"Immediately, M'sieu," the assistant undermanager said.

Prince, with a half-whine, a half-growl, and a

nudge of his enormous head, made his presence known.

"Well, little doggie," Matthew said. "You remember me, do you?" He reached out and scratched Prince's ears. The dog's tail began to wag. With one graceful sweep of his tail, he wiped the adjacent table clean of two full dinners, two wine coolers, and a twelve-candle candelabra. Matthew turned to see the source of the noise, and then picked up a crown of lamb from the floor and put it in the dog's mouth. The tail wagged again and there was the chilling sound of lamb bones crunching in Prince's enormous jaws.

"Dogs," Boris announced solemnly, "are fine judges of character. The last man who tried to feed Prince is still in the hospital."

"But he knows that I like him," Matthew said. "And I'm sure he remembers our first meeting. He took a playful nip at me, and I bit him back. Dogs remember things like that."

"I have just returned from Moscow," Boris said. "My triumphal return, however, has been marred by the callous desertion of my so-called friends."

"I know. It was on the front page of *Le Figaro*," Matthew replied. "You say that whatshisname, the Arab chap, and the ladies are in San Francisco?"

"They left me stranded, alone, and friendless in Moscow," Boris said.

"What an odd, unfortunate circumstance," Matthew said.

"How's that?"

"I came here from San Francisco specifically to take advantage of your offer," Matthew said.

"What offer was that? What were you doing in San Francisco? Did you see Baby Sister when you were there?"

"I will reply to your interrogatories in reverse order," Matthew said. "I did indeed see your charming sibling while in the City on the Bay. I shared a rather delightful repast with her and her husband—perhaps her consort would be the more apt word—at their home."

73

"And how is that little four-eyed jerk treating my baby sister?" Boris asked.

"They have found, it would appear, bliss in their marital union," Matthew said. "I confess I was quite touched by the sight of Radar* sitting on Kristina's lap, tenderly holding her left hand as she ran the fingers of her right hand lovingly through what little remains of his hair."

"My baby sister is a saint," Boris said, emotionally. "What she sees in that little twerp is beyond me."

"The second part of your multiple inquiry, if memory serves," Matthew Q. Framingham went on, "was to inquire what I was doing in San Francisco."

"Well?"

"I was there on Framingham Foundation** business," Mr. Framingham replied.

"Oh?"

"You are doubtless aware that it will shortly be time once again for the annual seminar on the dance," Mr. Framingham said.

"Wouldn't miss it for the world!" Boris said immediately.

"When you get right down to it, my dear friend, parts one and two of your interrogatory are interrelated," Matthew said. "Specifically, I went to San Francisco to engage a particular performer for the annual seminar on the dance, one Ms. Betsy Boobs."

"She's the one you told me about? The blonde with the fantastic jugs?"

"I wouldn't phrase it, being a Harvard man, in quite those terms, old bean, but her mammiform development is, in essence, the foundation of her appeal."

"And?"

---

* While serving as corporal and company clerk of the 4077th MASH during the Korean Unpleasantness, Mr. J. Robespierre O'Reilly became known as "Radar" after it became known that he was telepathic on occasion and could sometimes read minds.

** Mr. Framingham here referred to the Matthew Q. Framingham Theosophical Foundation of Cambridge, Mass., which was founded in 1863 for the furtherance of philosophy, science, and theology, and of which he was executive secretary.

"She has disappeared," Matthew Q. Framingham said.

"So what?" Boris asked. "What's one stripper, more or less, missing from the annual seminar on the dance? Last year we had eighteen, didn't we? Including the triplets?"

"Joan, Jeanne, and Josephine," Matthew recalled. "Six times the pleasure, six times the fun. They will be back, of course."

"Then what's so special about Betsy Boobs?" Boris asked.

"To get right to the crux of the matter, old chap, I am rather infatuated with the lady."

"Not again, Matthew!" Boris said. "I've told you and *told* you, don't become infatuated with strippers!"

"I can't help myself," Matthew said. "It is the cross I must bear on my path through life."

"You know what happened the last time," Boris said.

"What do you mean?"

"That brewer's daughter with the strange name . . ."

"Monica P. Fenstermacher, you mean?"

"She broke off her engagement to you because you were hung up on some stripper."

"That was time before last," Matthew said. "Last time . . . I'd rather not talk about last time."

"You should have learned your lesson by now," Boris said righteously.

"You're a fine one to talk, you with your Esmerelda," Matthew said.

"Esmerelda is a hoofer,"* Boris said. "There's a difference."

"Esmerelda prances around on a stage in very little clothing," Matthew said. "The only significant difference I can see between your Esmerelda and my Betsy Boobs is that the music is different."

"Maybe you have a point," Boris said. "How did you meet this one?"

* The reference here is to Esmerelda Hoffenburg, the ballerina. By "hoofer," Boris meant that she danced on the legitimate stage rather than in strip joints.

"I was out in San Francisco about a year ago," Matthew said. "And I just happened to drop in to this little place for a bite to eat and a moment's quiet reflection."

"What little place?"

"Sadie Shapiro's Strip Joint," Matthew said. "To be precise."

"And she was there?"

"She was there," Matthew said. "I fought it, Boris. You have to believe that. I told myself that sort of thing was all behind me, that it was a thing from my past, that if I ever hoped to regain Miss Monica P. Fenstermacher as my fiancée, I would have to put all the thoughts I was having from my mind."

"And?"

"It didn't work," Matthew said. "When I got back to Cambridge, I just couldn't put her from my mind. I began to send her little tokens of my esteem."

"Such as?"

"Flowers, candy, that sort of thing. Little trinkets."

"How often?"

"I didn't sign my name. I just had them include a card saying 'From an admirer.' "

"How *often,* Matthew?"

"Once a day," Matthew said.

"You sent her flowers, or a box of candy, or a little trinket *every* single day?"

"Flowers *and* candy *and* a little trinket every day," Matthew said. "But I didn't sign my name. I didn't want to overwhelm her, to frighten the little dove away."

"And?"

"Finally, I couldn't live with it any longer. I told myself that all I was doing was getting one more performer for the annual seminar on the dance, but in my heart of hearts, I knew that it was more than that, that I would declare myself as soon as I saw her again."

"So what happened?"

"When I got to San Francisco, I went there immediately. I mean, of course, after I checked into the

Mark Hopkins and changed clothes, and after I went by the Harvard Club. But as soon as humanly possible."

"And she wasn't there? So what? They change jobs all the time."

"I'm well aware of that," Matthew said. It came to his attention then that the two jeroboams of Piper Heidsieck '48 from which he and Boris had been sipping were empty. He summoned the manager.

"I would like some whiskey," he said. "I am in no mood at all to drink nothing but champagne."

"Either am I," Boris said. "Bring us each a bottle or two of whiskey."

"As I was saying," Matthew went on, "I thought it was simply a case of her having accepted another position. So I got in touch with her agent, and he told me that he had no idea where she was, that shortly after I had seen her, she had simply vanished from the face of the earth."

"You suspect foul play?"

"I checked that out, too. She has not been hospitalized, arrested, or gone to that great runway in the sky."

Boris thought of one more possibility, but kept it to himself in deference to his friend's sensitivities.

"Neither," Matthew said, making Boris wonder if Matthew was reading his mind, "has she taken out a marriage licence. I checked that, too."

"Well, is there any way I can help?"

"I did think you might have some idea how I should proceed, Boris. You're more experienced in these matters than I am."

"My experience, little buddy, is in running *away* from women, not after them."

"You have no suggestion to offer?"

"Indeed I do," Boris said as the waiter appeared with two half-gallons of Old Highland Dew Straight Scotch Whiskey. "Drink hearty."

"What else is there to do?" Matthew said, reaching for his half-gallon. "Betsy Boobs is lost to me forever."

At two the next afternoon, Boris Alexandrovich Korsky-Rimsakov was wakened from a sound sleep by a strangely annoying sound, part buzzing and part ringing.

"What in the hell is that awful noise?" he inquired rather loudly. There was no answer. After a moment, he recalled that he was quite alone in Paris, the miserable little camel jockey having run off to San Francisco with his *cercle intime* the moment his back was turned.

He groaned mightily and then sat up in bed. The dawn, as they say, came.

"It's the goddamned telephone," he announced. "That's what it is." He wondered, aloud, why no one had the common decency to answer it, and only moments afterward recalled, again, that he was deserted and quite alone and that, among other horrors, he was faced with the very real prospect of having to answer his own telephone. *God alone,* he mused, *knows what fool is on the other end of the line, daring to disturb the rest of the world's greatest opera singer.*

He picked up the telephone.

"Is this Boris Alexandrovich Korsky-Rimsakov, also known as El Noil Snoil the Magnificent?"

"Who wants to know?"

"This is the San Francisco, California, overseas operator, sir. I have a call for the guy with all those funny names from some nut who says he's calling for the Sheikh of Abzug. I was tempted to hang up on him, but I figured, what the hell, Ma Bell can use the money."

"Put him on," Boris said.

"It's collect, honey," the operator said.

"Then it must be Abdullah," Boris said.* "Hey, Abdullah, how they hanging?"

---

* From this point on, the conversation was carried on in Abzugian. It has been translated into English for those readers unfamiliar with that language, and also because no known type face is available for the printing of Abzugian, which consists in the main of grunts, wheezes, snorts, and a belch-like sound of exclamation.

"I am afraid that I have been a bad boy again, El Noil Snoil," His Royal Highness said.

"What now, Abdullah?"

"At first things went well. I saw your sister, and then I played poker with Radar and his friends."

"You didn't lose your temper again, did you, Abdullah? I *told* you it was a no-no to use your scimitar on people just because you lose."

"I was winning," His Royal Highness replied. "That makes the source of the difficulty."

"What difficulty?"

"I laid a full house—aces over three kings—on the table, and as you taught me, El Noil Snoil, I recited the sacred, time-honored words, 'Read 'em and weep, you bastards'—and then the skinny little gentleman was suddenly stricken with a very bad cough."

"What skinny little gentleman?"

"A person named Colonel Whiley."

"Well, some guys are good losers and some aren't. My experience has been that if you scratch a colonel, you get a lousy loser. So what?"

"Well, the other gentlemen, two doctors, were very upset about the whole thing, and they called for an ambulance and carried him away."

"Sometimes there are no lengths to which colonels will not go to get out of paying up, Abdullah," Boris philosophized. "But on the other hand, maybe he was sick. The question is, why tell me?"

"It is a sacred Abzugian custom, El Noil Snoil, that when someone falls ill at your table, you care for him."

"That wasn't your table, it was Radar's," Boris replied.

"But my aces over kings made him sick," the sheikh countered. "It is therefore my responsibility. And I can't find Radar."

"Where are you?"

"In a small set of rooms in someplace called the Mark Hopkins," the sheikh replied.

"Well, don't worry about it," Boris replied. "I will personally handle everything."

"You will?"

79

"Yes, I will. I'll get in touch with Hassan and have him pay the little guy's bill. What was that name again?"

"Whiley."

"My advice to you is to come back to Paris," Boris said.

"I could not do that until this matter is resolved."

"Whatever you say, Abdullah," Boris replied. "I'll get back to you."

"If I am not here, you may reach me at one of the local temples," the Sheikh said.

"Local temples?"

"There is this place called Sadie Shapiro's Strip Joint," the sheikh said. "I have rented it, girls and all, for as long as I will be here."

"I seem to have heard that name someplace before," Boris said. "It sounds very nice, Abdullah, and if I hadn't pushed myself to the very edge of exhaustion giving my artistic all to the Russian masses, I might even join you. But I need my rest. Have a good time."

"Mud in your eye, my friend," the sheikh said, courteously closing the conversation in English. The phone went dead.

Boris looked at the telephone a moment, and then dialed a number from memory.

"The Embassy of His Most Islamic Majesty, the Sheikh of Hussid," a foreign-sounding voice answered.

"This is Boris Alexandrovich Korsky-Rimsakov," Boris said. "I have just had a telephone call from San Francisco. I want you to get in touch with Prince Hassan, and tell him that Abdullah, his royal nibs, made somebody sick at a poker game, and that he'd better pay his bill. Got that?" He did not wait for a reply. He dropped the phone on its hook.

"God, the sacrifices I make every day for my fellow man!" he said.

He closed his eyes. In a moment, he was sound asleep again, his snores causing the crystal pendants on the chandeliers to rattle softly.

Chapter Six

Prince, who slept on an enormous red goatskin hassock (which had previously been in the harem of the Sheikh of Abzug, where Boris had seen it, admired it, and been made a present of it) placed near the foot of his master's bed, suddenly sat up, perked up his ears, moved with grace from the hassock to the side of the bed, and lapped his master's face with an enormous sandpapery tongue.

Boris Alexandrovich Korsky-Rimsakov, feeling Prince's loving, abrasive tongue on his face, woke with a groan and swung a massive fist at the dog, who nimbly avoided it, and then playfully pulled the covers off his master with his teeth.

"That's all I need!" Boris said. He thought that over. "What I really need is a cold shower!" he added. "Early to bed and early to rise, as I always say!"

Moving with exquisite care, so as not to disturb his brain (which was apparently rolling around inside his cranium like a bowling ball), he rose from his bed, and, supporting himself by holding onto the wall, made his way to the bath.

The bathroom had been a little gift to the world's greatest opera singer from His Royal Highness, Sheikh Abdullah ben Abzug. Where Boris had previously had to make do with a tub, a shower, a sink, and what the British call a w.c., like the rest of us, as a result of the sheikh's little gift he now had a sunken tub fifteen feet by twenty feet, from the center of which rose a gold-plated statue of a naked lady astride a dolphin. A stream from the dolphin's mouth served as the tub's source of water, the temperature and flow of which could be controlled by raising and lowering controls cleverly concealed in (more accurately, perhaps, disguised as) the naked lady's most obvious anatomical characteristics.

The walls and ceiling of the room were covered by etched mirrors; the etchings had been executed by a Czech émigré to the United States who had chosen as his theme the last days of the Pompeian baths. Separate rooms, hidden behind mirrored doors, provided access to water closets and other plumbing apparati. There were three such facilities—one for men, one for ladies, and one reserved for Boris. In this last, the apparati were somewhat oversized and were placed somewhat higher off the ground than is normal.

There were a sauna and a massage table too, of course. Taking a leaf from the Japanese notebook on comfort while bathing, a shower stall, with separate drainage facilities and eight shower heads, was off to one side.

Taps set into one wall of the bathroom dispensed beer, wine, soda water, and the bather's choice of Scotch, bourbon, cognac, or gin. A gold-plated object patterned after a Venetian funeral urn circulated iced water to cool champagne bottles. (The glasses, of course, as a safety measure, were all plastic. A rack to dispense them, à la Dixie cups, was mounted to the side of the taps.)

Boris reached the bathroom and stepped inside. Steeling himself for the effort, he stripped out of his silken dressing gown. He put his arms out to his sides, took a deep breath, and rushed to the bathtub, intending to enter the pool in a swan-dive. In his condition, unfortunately, his sense of balance was a bit off, and he entered the water sidewards. An enormous wave washed over the sides of the tub, splashed against the mirrored walls, and receded. The automatic water-level and temperature sensing controls were fooled by the wave, and the dolphin's mouth began to spit out a thick stream of water.

Boris came to the surface. The shock had brought him partly, but not entirely, to his senses. He floated quietly in the tub, grimacing at the noise of Prince's barking. Prince didn't like his master to leave him, but neither did he like the water. While he made up his mind what to do about it, he barked excitedly. The sound reverberated painfully off the mirrored walls and against Boris' eardrums.

Finally, choosing the side of loyalty over personal comfort, Prince leapt with a great bound into the tub, and swam (rather ungracefully, it must be reported) toward his beloved master.

Boris felt the splash and raised his head.

"Get out of my bathtub, you stupid mutt!" he bellowed.

In both exhaling and moving around, the singer lost buoyancy. He sank beneath the lightly scented waters of his tub. In a moment, he bobbed up again. Prince was standing up in the shallow end of the tub, looking at him with boundless love, his huge tail splashing water with each swing. And then Boris saw something else.

"What the hell?" Boris Alexandrovich Korsky-Rimsakov said. He shook his head as if to clear a mirage from his vision, and looked again at the corner of the bathroom in which the eight-headed shower stall stood. The apparition, or whatever it was, was still there. Standing under the flowing water of the shower was a rather handsome young man, quite naked. The index finger of his right hand was extended, and with it he poked in rapt fascination at his lower abdomen, about four inches above the junction of his legs.

"Who the hell are you?" Boris demanded. "And what are you doing in my bathroom? And stop whatever obscene gesture it is you're making! Prince is still a pup!"

"Good morning, *Cher* Maestro!" the young man

said, in rather oddly accented French. "I trust you slept well?"

At that moment, one of the mirrored doors opening onto the bathroom opened. A rather chubby female face, the kind that generally accompanies the body of females described by those friends and relatives who wish to pair them off with unsuspected new acquaintances as "a barrel of laughs," appeared at the edge of the door, said "Ooops!" and "Excuse *me*," and finally (and somewhat reluctantly, Boris thought) withdrew.

"Who the *hell* was *that?*" Boris asked. "And how dare she peer into my bathroom?"

"That's Imogene," the naked young man said. He poked again at his abdomen.

"I hope she saw what you're doing," Boris said. "Perhaps it will scare her away." He thought about that a moment, and changed his mind. "On second thought, it will probably drive her wild. So knock it off!"

He collected, as well as he was able, his thoughts. For the first time, he remembered that he had met Matthew Q. Framingham the previous evening.

"Framingham!" he bellowed, in the same voice that had less than twenty-four hours before caused the crystal pendants in the chandeliers of the Bolshoi Opera to rattle.

In the dining room of the apartment, Mr. Matthew Q. Framingham, who had chosen to retire for the evening under the Louis XVI dining table Boris had borrowed from the Palace of Versailles, was suddenly brought from a deep sleep by Boris' voice. He sat up as if someone had applied a cattle prod to his rear. Since the distance from his waist to the top of his head was greater than the distance between the floor and the bottom of the table, this served to give him a nasty crack on the head. As quickly as he had sat up, he lay down again, quite unconscious.

When there was no answer to his first summons, or his second, or his third, Boris Alexandrovich Korsky-Rimsakov rose from his bath like a surfacing whale, wrapped a towel around his loins, and stalked through the apartment. As he passed through the dining room, he saw Matthew Q. Framingham's size 12 D black wingtips sticking out from under the table. He reached down and grabbed both of them, pulling Mr. Framingham into sight.

"It'll do you no good to try to hide under there, you overgrown stripper freak!" he said, somewhat petulantly. "What have you done to me? How come there's a naked man in my bathroom and a fat lady named Imogene staring shamelessly at me while I bathe?"

Matthew Q. Framingham, who was unconscious, of course did not reply.

"My God!" Boris said. "He's dead!"

Matthew Q. Framingham groaned.

"If not dead, then dying!" Boris corrected himself. He snatched the telephone from the serving table and dialed a number.

"The Embassy of His Most Islamic Majesty, the Sheikh of Hussid," a voice with a British accent said.

"This is Boris Alexandrovich Korsky-Rimsakov," the singer said. "Is that you, Omar?"

"Good afternoon, Maestro," the charge d'affaires said. "How may I be of service?"

"Get your ass in high gear," Boris replied. "Get over here with an ambulance and the best medical attention you can find."

"I hear and obey, Maestro," the Charge d'Affaires replied. "Where is here?"

"My apartment," Boris said. "Hurry!" He slammed the phone down in its cradle. Then he bent over Matthew Q. Framingham and rather tenderly picked him up and carried him into his bedroom. He laid him gently on the bed.

"Whatever happened is obviously your fault, not mine," Boris said to the unconscious figure. "However, if you really do croak, I'll never hear the end of it."

"Is something wrong, Maestro?" the young man asked, coming into the room. He had a towel wrapped around his middle.

"I think he's dying," Boris said.

The young man went quickly to Matthew Q. Framingham and put his ear to his chest.

"What the hell are you doing?" Boris asked.

"His heart seems all right," the young man said. "Are you a doctor?"

"In the monastery of St. Igor, I was sometimes permitted to help the medical brothers in their work," the young man said.

Matthew groaned again. And there came, ever so faintly, the sound of sirens.

"Hi, there!" the lady named Imogene said. "Can I help?"

"Get out!" Boris shouted. "Can't you recognize a death bed when you see one?"

The sound of both the approaching sirens and Matthew's groans grew louder. And finally, as the sound of the sirens suddenly died (indicating that siren-bearing vehicles had reached their destination) and the sound of running feet on the steps could be heard, Matthew Q. Framingham opened one eye. He saw Boris standing over him and closed it.

"At the risk of being thought an unappreciative guest, old chap, I really do wish you would go away and come back later," he said. "I am in no condition whatever to attempt to get out of bed, much less to continue our revelry."

There was the sound of knocking at the apartment door, and Boris rushed to it.

Sheikh Omar ben Abdullah, chargé d'affaires of the Royal Hussidic Embassy, stood, somewhat out of breath, at the door, accompanied by two rather distinguished-looking French gentlemen in their middle years. Behind them stood four ambulance attendants bearing a stretcher.

"Are you all right, Maestro?" the chargé d'affaires asked with deep concern. "If anything happens to you while His Royal Highness is gone, he will never forgive me."

"Forgive you? He'd cut your head off, that's what he'd do! But it's not me. It's my dear and good friend

Matthew Q. Framingham. He's in there." He pointed to the bedroom door. "Wait a minute," he said. "Who are these guys?"

"Maestro, may I present Dr. Pierre St. Pierre, chief of staff of the Paris Municipal Hospital?"

"*Enchanté*, Maestro," Dr. St. Pierre said.

"And Dr. Francois de la Rougepied, professor of social diseases of the University of Paris."

"There's not a moment to be lost," Boris said, grabbing the medical gentlemen by the arms and propelling them toward the bedroom.

"It is a great honor, Maestro, to be of service to you," Dr. de la Rougepied said in French.

"Sorry to disappoint you, Doc," Boris said. "But as I said, it's not me. It's my l'il buddy, Framingham."

"And what seems to be wrong with him?" Omar asked.

"How the hell should I know?" Boris said. "That's what the docs are here for." He thrust open the door and gestured at the bed. "There he is, Doc."

Matthew Q. Framingham was now fully awake, if still a little groggy. He attempted to sit up in the bed.

"Let me help you!" the young man in the towel said, and he did so, bending over the bed and lifting Matthew to a semierect position against the headboard.

Dr. Pierre St. Pierre and Dr. de la Rougepied both examined Mr. Framingham, and then exchanged glances, nods, and profound grunts.

"Maestro," Dr. de la Rougepied began.

"Zair is no-zing wrong wiff your fren," Dr. St. Pierre picked up.

"He has giff himself, what you zay, one hell of a crack on zee head," Dr. de la Rougepied continued.

"And he has, of course, one hell of a hang-ovair," Dr. St. Pierre went on.

"But no-zing zat requires zee services of a docteur," Rougepied concluded.

"Thank God!" Boris said.

"On zee ozair hand," Dr. Rougepied said.

"Zeez young man is, what you say, a horze of zee

other color," Dr. St. Pierre said, pointing at the young man in the towel.

"What the hell are you talking about?" Boris asked.

"I happened to look under his towel," Dr. de la Rougepied said.

"God, your kind are all over!"

"An' I call what I zee to zee attention of my colleague," Rougepied went on.

"And I zee zee zame zing," St. Pierre added.

"Couple of lousy voyeurs," Boris said. "Thank God I have my pants on, otherwise you two would be uncontrollable."

"And what we zee is obviously what you call an inguinal hernia," Dr. de la Rougepied said.

"My God!" Boris said. "I must think of my public! Exactly how contagious is that, Doctor?"

"It is what you call zee *rapture*," Dr. St. Pierre said.

"I believe the word you seek, sir," Sheikh Abdullah said, "is rupture, not rapture."

"Ruptured," Dr. de la Rougepied said in French. "And recently, too. He has obviously picked up an enormous load within the past twelve hours."

"I really don't care, when you get right to it," Boris said. "I don't even know who the hell he is."

"Boris, your conduct is unspeakable!" Matthew Q. Framingham said. "Have you no small shred of appreciation, much less gratitude, for what this young man has done for you?"

"Huh?"

"That enormous load to which the doctor refers?"

"What about it?"

"It was *you*," Matthew said. "This splendid young chap carried you in here last night."

"I never saw this guy in my life until he showed up in my bathroom and started making obscene gestures at my dog!" Boris said. He looked at the young man, who was again prodding his abdomen with his finger. "See, there he goes again!"

"When one is suffairing from zee inguinal hernia," Dr. de la Rougepied said, "zee symptom one zees first is zee bulge in zee lower abdomen. Zat is what he is doing now. It is of no avail. Everytime he push it in, it will pop out again."

"What has any of this to do with me?" Boris said. "I never saw this guy before!"

"But, Boris, you did!" Matthew said. "Don't you remember being in the Casanova last night?"

"Of course I do," Boris said. "I remember quite clearly giving you wise fatherly counsel about this stripteaser fetish of yours."

"And you do recall the balalaika player?"

"Of course I do," Boris said. "He was, as I recall, superb."

"And do you remember asking him to join us?"

"Of course I do. What are you leading up to, Framingham?"

"And taking him with us, when we were asked to leave the Casanova, to the Ritz Bar?"

"How could I possibly forget something like that? The balalaika player was a great musical artist."

"I'm glad you remember that," Framingham said, "because you will then probably remember that after we were asked to leave the Ritz Bar—"

"*We* were asked to leave the Ritz Bar?" Boris asked incredulously.

"That was after you were challenged to a duel by that Argentinian chap who felt you were paying undue attention to his wife."

"I offended someone's wife?" Boris asked. "Impossible."

"She wasn't offended," Matthew said.

"That's better," Boris said.

"But her husband objected when you suggested that the two of you get a room and, as you somewhat indelicately put it, give the ol' springs a workout."

"I'm sure you're mistaken," Boris said.

"He said he would send his seconds to see you this afternoon," Matthew said, "but we digress. After we left the Ritz, we went to Harry's Bar, and there you told the balalaika player that, being the greatest one of all, you recognized a musical genius whenever you saw one."

"I recall something of that," Boris said.

"And you told him that his problems—"

"What problems?"

"He is alone and penniless in Paris."

"Oh."

"Were over. That you would make him your protégé and get him a scholarship."

"I said that, did I?" Boris said. "Well, if I said it, I must have meant it. Abdullah?"

"Yes, El Noil Snoil the Magnificent?"

"Get this young man's name, and tell Hassan I said to give him a scholarship."

"Of course, El Noil Snoil."

"And once that was out of the way, we went to the American Legion," Matthew Q. Framingham said. "Do you remember that?"

"Not too clearly," Boris confessed. "It had been a trying day."

"Well, we went to the American Legion," Matthew Q. Framingham said. "There we met Imogene."

"Imogene?" Boris asked. "Who the hell is Imogene?"

"Did I hear someone call me?" the chubby lady said, peeking around the door.

"Out! Out!" Boris cried. "Have you no decency? Can't you see that this young man is virtually at death's door?" He then turned to Matthew Q. Framingham. "Get out of the bed and let this guy lie down, Matthew! That's the trouble with you Harvard types. Always thinking about yourselves!"

"You suggested to Imogene and her friend—"

"My God, there's more than one?"

"Two," Matthew said. "They're from Chillicothe, Ohio."

"I am beginning to suspect, Matthew, that you took advantage of my innocent nature and got me drunk again," Boris said. "You should really be ashamed of yourself, Matthew."

"Well, when we got here, you were asleep."

"No surprise. I was exhausted. Didn't I tell you that I had come to Paris directly from a triumphal performance in Moscow? And that I had very nearly been starved to death in Moscow?"

"In any event, when we reached here, you were unconscious. And this splendid young man carried you upstairs, obviously rupturing himself in the process."

"That simply goes to show what happens to people who butt in," Boris said. "Carrying me upstairs is the responsibility of Hassan's bodyguard. Where the hell were they?"

"They were protecting you from the brothers of the lady from Argentina," Matthew said. "They had followed us all the way to the American Legion. We had to go out by the back door."

"Well, at least they were meeting their responsibilities," Boris said. "Which is more than I can say for you, Matthew. Why didn't *you* carry me upstairs?"

"I was somewhat *hors de combat* myself," Matthew confessed. "As a matter of fact it was necessary for Imogene and her friend to assist me."

"And this little guy," Boris said, examining the young man closely, "actually carried me up three flights of stairs?"

"My pleasure, dear Boris," the young man said.

"There is simply nothing beyond us musical geniuses, is there?" Boris said. "And never let it be said that Boris Alexandrovich Korsky-Rimsakov doesn't pay his debts. First things first, however. Abdullah, where is the bodyguard?"

"They are outside, El Noil Snoil," Abdullah replied.

"Have them escort the ladies to their hotel," Boris said. "Or anywhere else they might wish to go. But get them out of here. Whatever will my neighbors think?"

"Your wish is my command, El Noil Snoil," Abdullah replied.

"And don't you forget it," Boris said. He turned to Dr. de la Rougepied. "You say this fellow has a hernia?"

"Yes, Maestro," the doctor replied in French.

"How does one treat a hernia?"

"With surgery, Maestro," Dr. de la Rougepied re-

91

plied. "He will require surgery. But have no fear, Maestro. I have a colleague who is professor of surgery at the University of Paris Medical School. He will, I am sure, consider it an honor to attend to any friend of our *Cher* Boris, the world's greatest opera singer."

"Well, I'm sure he would," Boris replied. "But if you think I'm going to let some French chancre-mechanic put a knife to *my* benefactor and protégé, think again!"

"I beg pardon, Maestro?"

"Omar, you did bring an ambulance?"

"Two, Maestro," the chargé d'affaires replied. "Just in case."

"Have this lad loaded aboard one," Boris ordered. "Gentle, now, he gave his all for me. Greater love hath no man, so to speak, than to rupture himself helping Boris Alexandrovich Korsky-Rimsakov in his hour of need."

"I'll call the hospital and reserve a room," Dr. de la Rougepied said.

"Nothing personal, Doc," Boris said, "but nothing is too good for this young musical genius and protégé of mine."

"I don't quite follow you," Dr. de la Rougepied said.

"There's no such thing as second-best," Boris replied. "And Pancho here gets the best." He picked up the telephone. "Operator, connect me with Dr. Benjamin Franklin Pierce at the Spruce Harbor Medical Center in Maine." He covered the phone with his hand. "Call the airport, Abdullah, and have the engines started!"

Chapter Seven

When it was three-thirty in the afternoon in Paris, it was half-past ten in the morning in Spruce Harbor, Maine. When the telephone rang in the office of the chief of surgery, that luminary, dressed in fresh surgical greens, was in his office taking a brief rest between what it is now chic to refer to as surgical procedures (formerly known as "operations," which should, by all rules of logic, be known as "cutting, tying and sewing-ups").

The previous surgical procedure had been one known to the layman and to Dr. Pierce as "jerking a gall-bladder," a fairly routine thing to occur under Dr. Pierce's scalpel. The jerking in question, however, had been an unusual one, posing certain problems and requiring certain out-of-the-ordinary steps.

So, instead of spending his restbreak as it was his custom to—sipping on black coffee and keeping up with the latest anatomical developments (as published in *Penthouse* and such other magazines of the literary and cultural establishment)—Dr. Pierce was spending it sipping on black coffee and explaining what had happened in the operating room to Student Nurse Barbara Ann Miller.

It was not his custom to take student nurses under his wing, but Barbara Ann Miller was, in Dr. Pierce's professional opinion (which was shared by Dr. McIntyre and chief of nursing services Esther Flanagan), that *rara avis,* a young woman with an obvious potential for becoming one hell of a good operating-room nurse.

Student Nurse Miller, who would graduate in June, had come to the Spruce Harbor Medical Center as a transfer student from the Ms. Prudence MacDonald Memorial School of Nursing of New Orleans, La. Her transcript of grades had born a notation from the Reverend Mother Superior Bernadette of Lourdes, M.D., F.A.C.S., chief of staff of the Gates of Heaven Hospital of New Orleans, to the effect that it was *her* personal judgement that Miss Miller showed the potential to become one hell of an operating-room nurse.

Student Nurse Miller had not begun her nursing education at Gates of Heaven, either, but rather at San Francisco's Pacific General Hospital. The details of her transfer from San Francisco to New Orleans and then to Spruce Harbor were a carefully kept secret, known only to the Reverend Mother Superior Bernadette of Lourdes; Doctors Pierce and McIntyre; Esther Flanagan, R.N.; and Margaret Houlihan Wachauf Wilson, R.N., chief of nursing instruction of the Ms. Prudence MacDonald Memorial School of Nursing.

There was more to Margaret H. W. Wilson, R.N., the chief of nursing instruction at the Ms. Prudence MacDonald Memorial School of Nursing, than her name implied. The nursing school occupied but half her time, professionally speaking. Like the Reverend Mother Superior Bernadette of Lourdes, M.D., F.A.C.S., of Gates of Heaven, Nurse Wilson divided her professional life between medicine and the church.

It was not, however, the same church. Nurse Wilson was associated with the God Is Love In All Forms Christian Church, Inc., which had been founded in San Francisco, California, several years before by her late husband, the Reverend Buck Wilson, as a churchly refuge for those who, for one reason or another, did not feel quite at home, or comfortable, or even welcome, in any of the then-established persuasions.*

---

* *The Official History of the God Is Love in All Forms Christian Church, Inc.,* for those interested in what is described as "the new theology," is available from the Headquarters Temple, GILIAFCC, Inc., 209 Bourbon Street, New Orleans, La. 70007 for $49.95 (illustrated, with hymnal).

94

Shortly after Buck Wilson's untimely and premature passing,** his widow was named by the founding disciples of the church to the newly created position of Reverend Mother Emeritus. Although her position as such was first thought of as purely ceremonial, the Widow Wilson quickly assumed a genuine role of leadership within the church hierarchy. Within a matter of months, it was generally conceded that she and she alone held the reins, and held them a good deal more firmly than her late husband ever had.***

It was she, for example, who had flatly forbidden the God Is Love in All Forms Christian Church, Inc., all-male a capella choir to wear eyeshadow and lipstick, and had made the prohibition stick.

In addition to her administrative skills and a hitherto repressed and unused maternal understanding and compassion for what she came to think of as "her boys," Margaret Houlihan Wachauf **** Wilson brought to GILIAFCC, Inc., a certain presence and image.

The years had been kind to her, physically speaking. She was an imposing lady, made even more imposing by her churchly vestments. These had been designed for her as a joint effort by two of the founding disciples who happened to be designers of lady's high-fashion

Those either pressed for funds or interested in a somewhat more objective view of the organization will find it described with some skill and style in *M*A*S*H Goes to New Orleans*, *M*A*S*H Goes to Paris*, and *M*A*S*H Goes to Las Vegas* (Pocket Books, New York) $1.50 each. The GILIAFCC, Inc., offers a thirty-five-percent discount to the clergy, divinity students, and *bona fide* theological scholars. Pocket Books does not.

** The Reverend Buck Wilson expired of heart failure (said to be brought about by exhaustion) on the nuptial couch. While there is some controversy concerning this, the death mask (copies of which, in Durastone, are available from the Headquarters Temple, GILIAFCC, Inc., at $11.95—$15.95 in goldplate) made at the time show him to be smiling.

*** The Reverend Wilson is reliably reported to have suffered from a limp wrist, and this possibly had some bearing on the problem.

**** Rev. Mother Emeritus Margaret Wilson was also the widow of the late Mr. Isadore Wachauf, founder and chairman of Wachauf Metal Recycling Corporation, International (formerly Izzy's junkyard). He had come to an early, tragic, and somewhat messy end shortly after their marriage when the electric power failed as Mr. Wachauf was standing under and examining an electromagnetic hoist in one of his yards. The electromagnet had been holding twenty tons of crushed automobiles when the juice went off.

clothing. Over a silver lamé gown with a rather low-cut bodice, the official vestments consisted of a purple cape lined in red velvet and featuring an ermine collar. Across the back of the cape, in sequins, was a large cross, reaching from the area of the shoulder blades to the ground. The word "Reverend" was spelled out on the vertical member of the cross and the words "Mother" and Emeritus" on the horizontal members.

Her headgear was based on the cappa magna made popular by bishops of the Roman Catholic Church. The Rev. Mother Emeritus Wilson was a very close personal friend of His Eminence John Joseph Mulcahy, titular Archbishop of Swengchan, a member of what is somewhat irreverently referred to as "the Pope's Kitchen Cabinet," whom she had first met when both were assigned to the 4077th MASH during the Korean War. (His Eminence had then been but a lowly priest and Army chaplain.) While visiting the archbishop in his apartment in Rome, she had playfully donned his cappa magna, and had instantly seen what it could signify to her flock.

So as not to be confused with a cleric of the Roman persuasion, the Reverend Mother Emeritus' cappa magna was chartreuse, rather than off-white, and—at no small expense—the flat surfaces, front and rear, had been cleverly wired so that the timeless truth "God Is Love" flashed on and off at five-second intervals, utilizing small red, white, and blue neon bulbs to spell out the letters.

On her left-hand ring finger, the Reverend Mother Emeritus wore a forty-two-carat square-cut diamond ring that had been presented to her by His Royal Highness Sheikh Abdullah ben Abzug as a small token of his appreciation for her having established the nursing and midwifery services of the Boris Alexandrovich Korsky-Rimsakov Memorial Lying-In Hospital in Abzug's capital. It had become the custom of the GILI-AFCC, Inc., for both senior church officials (such as the founding disciples) and new recruits to kiss the Star of Abzug, as the diamond was known, as a symbol of their recognition of Reverend Mother Emeritus as their shepherdess. (On such ceremonial occasions, the Reverend Mother Emeritus also carried the traditional ecclesiastical symbol of the churchly shepherd, a shepherd's crook—in other words, a pole with a curved-over top end.)

And finally, the Reverend Mother Emeritus wore—suspended from a stout gold chain about her neck—another cross, the vertical member approximately ten inches long, with the words "Mother" and "Emeritus" spelled out in diamonds, and the word "Reverend" spelled out in square-cut rubies. The dimensions of the cross and its weight usually caused the Reverend Mother Emeritus' bosoms to be brought into prominence as the chain dipped into the valley between them. While most of the Reverend Mother Emeritus' good works took place in New Orleans, Louisiana, at the Headquarters Temple of the GILIAFCC, Inc., she participated in the four annual pilgrimages. Of these, the most important was the "Back to the Beginning Pilgrimage" to San Francisco, California.

It had been at a table in Finocchio's Restaurant in San Francisco that the man now known as the blessed Brother Buck had held The First Supper, at which he and the twelve founding disciples had brought the God Is Love in All Forms Christian Church, Inc., to life. The Blessed Brother Buck, who before the call had been one of San Francisco's most sought-after male models and escorts, had come to the prayerful conclusion that it was his duty to found a church for those whom other organized religious bodies ignored or condemned vigorously.

To quote from the *Official History:* "The first dozen members, known as the founding disciples, included a fine artist, two hairdressers, a writer, two ballet dancers, a male model, two interior decorators, and the quarterback and two defensive tackles of the San Francisco Gladiators professional football team."

Shortly after its organization, partly because the Blessed Brother Buck (possibly in error) thought New Orleans would provide a more fertile field for his mis-

sionary labors than San Francisco, and partly because
the move was encouraged and financially underwrit-
ten by two affluent new converts, International Headquarters was moved to the Crescent City. Two founding
disciples (one of the defensive tackles and the writer,
who had just signed a long-term lease on what they
described as a "darling" apartment) remained behind
to establish the First Missionary Church of GILI-
AFCC, Inc. Annually, the "Back to the Beginning Pilgrimage" was made, headed by the Blessed Brother
Buck and, later, by his widow.

Over the years, this most important pilgrimage had
become a rather elaborate affair. There were welcoming ceremonies at the airport when the Reverend
Mother Emeritus, her entourage, the Founding Disciples who could make it, and the GILIAFCC, Inc.,
all-male a capella choir arrived.

A motorcade to First Church, as it was popularly
known, followed the welcoming ceremonies. The same
evening, a Memorial First Supper was held in Finocchio's Restaurant, following which there was a procession through the San Francisco entertainment district
to the Embarcadero. Led by Papa Louis' Old-Time
New Orleans Dixieland Jazz Band, the procession included the Reverend Mother Emeritus—in full regalia
—sitting in a gilt-covered chair (which was borne on
the shoulders of twelve of the more muscular devotees),
and the a capella choir. The faithful and their friends
brought up the rear.

As the procession proceeded along the streets, with
the Old-Time Jazz Band playing "We Will Gather At
The River," "Amazing Grace," "There'll Be a Hot
Time in the Old Town Tonight," and other such in-
spirational numbers, the Reverend Mother Emeritus
alternately raised her hand in blessing and threw gold-
plated coin-shaped discs (patterned after New Orleans'
famous Mardi Gras doubloons) bearing the likeness
of the Blessed Brother Buck to the cheering multi-
tudes.

From time to time, the procession would leave the
streets and pass through one or more commercial

enterprises along the route. A number of converts had been made in this way. There was something magical, in a circus sense, about the procession, and joining the procession (which was generally held a-round midnight) often struck many lost souls as far more promising than remaining hung over a bar stool watching the strippers.

After the procession reached the Embarcadero, it was the Reverend Mother Emeritus' custom to quietly disappear. If the Romans could have their Mardi Gras, she reasoned, there was no reason at all that her flock shouldn't have an excuse to kick up their heels once a year, too. But she knew that her presence at such revelry would only put a damper on things, so she slipped away as soon as she could at the end of the procession.

And so it came to pass, as it says in the Good Book, that one night a rather striking lady wearing a cape, and with what looked like a chartreuse Bishop's cappa magna tucked under her arm, strode into the bar at the Mark Hopkins Hotel, took a seat, and informed the bartender that she would like a triple martini, very easy on the vermouth, and save the olives for the vegetarians and other health-food nuts. As she gave the order, the lady heard a shocked intake of breath, but paid no attention to it. There were still, she knew, some people who presumed that a woman alone in a bar was looking for a man.

But when she had drained the triple martini at a gulp and handed the empty glass back to the bartender for a refill, and there came again the sound of a shocked intake of breath, together with a mumbled "Hypo-crite," it was too much for her female curiosity. She reached into a pocket of the cape, took out her glasses, and turned toward the sound of the sucked-in breath.

There was a modestly dressed young woman sitting on a bar stool glowering at her.

"Were you speaking to me, Sister?" the Reverend Mother Emeritus asked.

"You should be ashamed of yourself!" the young woman said.

"Probably," Reverend Mother Emeritus replied. "But I gather you have something specific in mind?"

"I saw you tonight!" the young woman said.

"And now that you mention it," Reverend Mother Emeritus replied, "I saw you earlier tonight, too. You were wearing a lot fewer clothes at the time. In an establishment called, if memory serves, Sadie Shapiro's Strip Joint."

"*You* were in some kind of far-out religious procession," the young woman went on, "dressed up like a bishop. And here you are in a bar, swilling martinis!"

"You have no idea, honey," the Reverend Mother Emeritus replied, "how tiring it is to get hauled around for hours on the shoulders of twelve men. I am simply following Saint Timothy's suggestion, First Timothy, chapter five, verse twenty-three, to take a little wine for my stomach's sake and my other infirmities."

"Huh!" the young woman snorted.

"Anyway, I had *my* clothes on," the Reverend Mother Emeritus said. "Which is more than I can say for some people."

"I'm working my way through nursing school," the young woman said.

"Ha!" the Reverend Mother Emeritus snorted disbelievingly. "That's a likely story."

"If there was the slightest possibility that you knew anything at all about medicine, about the training of nurses, I would explain it to you, but under the circumstances—'Some are already turned aside after Satan'—that's also First Timothy—chapter five, verse fifteen—it would be a waste of my time."

"I'll have you know," the Reverend Mother Emeritus said, raising her voice and getting to her feet, "that I have *forgotten* more about nursing than you can ever learn, you somewhat clumsy stripper!"

"Clumsy stripper! I'll have you know that I'm so good I have a fan who sends me a dozen long-stemmed roses, a box of Fanny Farmer's Genuine Old Creole Pecan Crispies, and a little trinket *every day*." She paused and held out her wrist, which bore the very latest digital light-emitting diode wristwatch. *"That kind of a trinket. This is today's trinket. Yesterday, it was an electric blanket to keep me comfy and cozy, the note said, when my act is over. That's how clumsy a stripper I am!"*

"Speaking professionally," the Reverend Mother Emeritus said, "as a nurse, I mean, with what you've got to shake, honey, you don't need much talent!"

"What do you mean, speaking as a nurse?"

"You heard me, honey—R.N., as in Registered by God Nurse!" the Reverend Mother Emeritus said, slight pique appearing in her otherwise dulcet tones.

"You? A nurse? That's a laugh!"

Reverend Mother Emeritus hiked up the skirt of her silver lamé gown. Strapped to her leg, above the knee, was a sort of purse. From it, she took a leather wallet. The silver lamé gown (more properly, cassock) was form-fitting, and there was noplace on or in it for a wallet or anything else that a lady might need.

"Have a look at that!" she said triumphantly.

The wallet was handmade. On one side, a medical caduceus, superimposed on the insignia of the United States Tenth Army Corps (Group), had been carved; below this was the word "Korea." The other side bore the carved legend, "Presented to Major Hot Lips Houlihan, U.S. Army Nurse Corps, by the boys in Ward Three."

The well-bosomed blonde looked at it intently. "How do I know this is yours?" she asked.

"Open it up, open it up," the Reverend Mother Emeritus snapped. When opened, the billfold revealed a fan of plastic envelopes, each holding, back to back, two photographs.

The blonde looked at the photographs, and then back at the Reverend Mother Emeritus. The years had taken their toll, of course, but there was no question that the Army nurse in the photographs was the woman sitting beside her. One of the photographs showed her in surgical greens posing with two tall chaps and a somewhat smaller one, similarly clad. The nurse in the picture had an arm draped around the smaller man.

"That's Dago Red," the Reverend Mother Emeritus said, pointing with a long fingernail painted with gold-flecked purple nail polish to the smaller fellow. "Now the Archbishop of Swengchan. Ask him whether I'm a nurse or not!"

Her fingernail moved to the other two men in the photograph. "And that's Dr. Hawkeye Pierce, now chief of surgery of the Spruce Harbor Medical Center. And the other one is Dr. Trapper John McIntyre, the second-best chest cutter north of Boston and east of Chicago. Ask either of *them*, why don't you!"

The blonde flipped through the rest of the photographs. They showed the woman now sitting beside her in a variety of situations. There was one showing her poised like the Statue of Liberty (instead of a torch, she held a bottle of Scotch) atop a Russian T-34 tank. Others showed her in a hospital. The last photograph showed her in a Jeep. On the back of that was a red Department of Defense identification card, issued to Houlihan, Margaret J., Lt. Colonel, Army Nurse Corps, Retired.

"I owe you an apology," the blonde said. "I'm really sorry."

"You damned well should be," the Reverend Mother Emeritus said. "Telling someone like me that you're working your way through nursing school by prancing around the bar in Sadie Shapiro's Strip Joint taking off your clothes."

"But that's true," the blonde said. "I *am* studying nursing. I hope to graduate in a year."

"Then what are you doing in Sadie Shapiro's?"

"Earning my way," the blonde said. "I told you before."

"Where I come from, they have such things as scholarships," the Reverend Mother Emeritus said suspiciously, but the white fire of her enraged pride had visibly cooled—it now merely smouldered menacingly.

"The truth of the matter is . . . what do I call you?"

"You call me Reverend Mother, that's what you damned well call me," that worthy replied.

"The truth of the matter, Reverend Mother, is that before I knew what I was meant to be in life, I was already a stripper."

"I see."

"And you can imagine how the scholarship committees reacted when they came to the spot on the form that asked about previous employment."

"Yes, I can," the Reverend Mother Emeritus said, now very much softened. "Tell me . . . what's your name?"

"Betsy Boobs," the young blonde said, and then, hurriedly, "Oh, you mean my real name. Barbara Ann Miller."

"How are you doing in nursing school, Barbara Ann? Grade-wise, I mean. That sort of thing."

"I have an A—average. I hope to become an operating room nurse, and I try as hard as I can," Barbara Ann replied. "What kind of nurse were you?"

"I *am* an operating-room nurse," the Reverend Mother Emeritus said. "Tell me, Barbara, can't your parents help you out?"

"I don't have any parents," Barbara Ann replied.

"Would you mind if I checked on your story?" the Reverend Mother Emeritus asked. Without waiting for a reply, she snapped her fingers to catch the bartender's attention. "Give me a phone, Charley," she ordered. "And set the little lady and me up again."

The waiter delivered the telephone, and the Reverend Mother got the number of the hospital from Barbara Ann, dialed it, and drummed her fingers impatiently. It was not possible to tell whether the impatience was with regard to the time it took the hospital to answer the telephone or the time it took the bartender to mix the martinis.

"Give me the chief of nursing services," she said to the telephone. "Margaret H. W. Wilson, chief nurse, the MacDonald School of Nursing, calling." Pause. "Yes, I know what time it is. What's the matter, don't you have a watch?" Pause, this time a long one. "'Sorry to bother you this time of night, but I felt it necessary," she began. "My name is Margaret H. W. Wilson, R.N., chief nurse, MacDonald School of Nursing." Pause. "Oh, you've heard of us? Good. Then you know we're associated with the Gates of Heaven Hospital, right?" Pause. "What I need is some information, out of school, about one of your students. A girl named Barbara Ann Miller." This time there was a long, long pause, during which the Reverend Mother nodded her head from time to time, but said nothing.

Finally, however, she spoke again. "Well, your problems about *that* are over. First thing in the morning, you send all her records to us. You can consider her transferred as of right now." Pause. "I'm sure there won't be any trouble, even though Gates of Heaven does have a religious connection. Not only have I got a religious connection myself, but the Archbishop owes me a couple of favors. There will be no trouble, you can take my word for it. Nice to talk to you." She put the telephone down, picked up her martini glass, and touched it to the martini glass in Barbara Miller's hand.

"Welcome to the Ms. Prudence MacDonald Memorial School of Nursing," she said.

"Is this for real?" Barbara Ann asked.

"You can take my word for it, honey. Would the Reverend Mother Emeritus fool around about something as important as this?"

Chapter Eight

It did not go quite as smoothly as the Reverend Mother Emeritus had believed it would. From the very first, Barbara Ann Miller was anything but a typical anonymous student nurse.

When the GILIAFCC, Inc., pilgrims returned to the Crescent City, bringing Barbara Ann with them, they were greeted by members of the news media—not particularly because their return was of such earth-shaking importance, but because Colonel Beauregard C. Beaucoupmots, publisher of the New Orleans *Picaroon-Statesman* and owner of WOOM–TV ("The Voice of the Cradle of the Confederacy"), was one of the Reverend Mother Emeritus' greatest admirers.

His admiration was not for her theological achievements nor for her medical skills. Colonel Beauregard Beaucoupmots was enamored of the lady he called "Miss Margaret" as a *lady*. He had first encountered her at the final rites of the Blessed Brother Buck. When she had spread her arms wide in a final gesture to the mourners, a strong gust of wind from Lake Ponchartrain had pressed her gown tightly against her body. The colonel hadn't seen such an exciting sight since he was fourteen, when his father had taken him to see Sally Rand and her Dance of the Bubbles at the New York World's Fair of 1939–40. As soon as what he considered to be a decent interval had passed (that is to say, the next day), he had proposed marriage. Upon rejection, he had repeated the offer to take her as his bride on the average of once every eighteen hours ever since, and showed no signs of discouragement whatever.

If getting publicity for either the GILIAFCC, Inc. (which organization the colonel referred to privately as "Miss Margaret's faggots"), or the Ms. Prudence MacDonald Memorial School of Nursing was the way to Miss Margaret's heart, then the *Picaroon-Statesman* and WOOM–TV were at her service.

Although there had been at first some resistance from the editor about such round-the-clock coverage of the GILIAFCC, Inc., it had soon passed. The editor learned that his readers were far more interested in reading about the day-to-day undertakings of the GILIAFCC, Inc., membership than they were in, for example, the things columnists Evans and Novak wrote about. Evans and Novak seldom provided a smile, much less hysterical laughter.

And so, when the door of the airplane opened, and the Reverend Mother Emeritus emerged to raise her shepherd's crook and offer a blessing to the inhabitants of the Crescent City, the ladies and gentlemen of the print and electronic media were on hand. Their cameras saw, and their sharp little pencils recorded, the new addition to the Reverend Mother Emeritus' entourage.

In the mistaken belief that Miss Barbara Ann Miller was a member of the GILIAFCC, Inc., faithful, four reporters, two cameramen, and the anchorman of the seven-thirty news—none of whom had been inside a church in a decade—showed up that same day at the International Headquarters Temple begging for admission.

When the photograph showing Miss Barbara Ann Miller standing behind the Reverend Mother Emeritus was printed in the evening edition of the *Picaroon-Statesman,* and the edition, in the quaint cant of the trade, "hit the streets," there were so many would-be applicants for membership in the GILIAFCC, Inc., milling around Bourbon Street that horse-mounted police were required to maintain order.

It cannot be said that the Reverend Mother Emeri-

106

tus did not do her best to dispel the interest in her transfer nursing student and to permit her to pursue her nursing studies in peace and quiet. But even the loan of twelve sturdy Knights of the Bayou Perdu Council, Knights of Columbus, guarding the doors of both the MacDonald School of Nursing and the Gates of Heaven Hospital were of no avail in keeping out the hordes of Miss Miller's admirers.

The straw that, so to speak, broke the back of the Reverend Mother Emeritus' firm intentions was the identification of Miss Barbara Ann Miller as Betsy Boobs. This was made by several New Orleans men whom business had taken to San Francisco.

It was impossible to continue nursing instruction in, say, "sutures, their application and removal" when the streets outside the classroom were filled with hordes of young (and old) men screaming, "We Want Betsy Boobs!" and "Take it off! Take it off! Take it off!"

It was at this point that Margaret H. W. Wilson, in her role as chief of nursing instruction, turned again to her old comrades-in-arms, Doctors Hawkeye Pierce and Trapper John McIntyre, and their chief nurse (and her friend), Esther Flanagan, R.N.

It was not that the young men of Spruce Harbor, Maine, would be immune to Barbara Ann Miller's charms, but rather that they were all too familiar, from painful experience, with the Scottish wolfhound* owned by Nurse Flanagan, chief of nursing services at Spruce Harbor and semi-official housemother of the nurses' dormitory there.

It could be said, and indeed was said, that the virtue of a young woman resident in the Spruce Harbor nurses' dorm was as safe as (probably safer than) it was at home. Very few fathers, after all, no matter how dark their suspicions, are able to detect their

---

* This was a litter mate of Prince, Boris Alexandrovich Korsky-Rimsakov's canine companion. How Mr. Korsky-Rimsakov and Nurse Flanagan came into possession of these animals has been reported, with careful attention to fact and the principles of animal husbandry, in *M*A*S*H Goes to Vienna* (Pocket Books, New York).

daughter's foul-intentioned suitors' presence in the bushes simply by smell, much less to instill the fear of God in them by growling and holding them down with a foot in the middle of their chests.

And so Senior Student Nurse Barbara Ann Miller, her semi-lurid past known only to Doctors Pierce and McIntyre and Nurse Flanagan, became a member of the Spruce Harbor student nursing body, and within a matter of weeks, despite all their efforts to resist, became the favorite of these three senior staff personnel.

In fairness, it must be stated that in the professional judgement of all three, Student Nurse Miller showed every indication of becoming, in Dr. Pierce's words, "the finest kind of cutting-room helper."

Nurse Flanagan once confided to Dr. McIntyre (after her fifth martini) that Barbara Ann reminded her very much of herself in her youth, "with all the guys panting after me."

So far as Doctors Pierce and McIntyre were concerned, what they referred to as Barbara Miller's "extracurricular activity" in San Francisco had given her at least one ability not often found in student nurses. She could make a martini of such ice-cold perfection and earth-moving effect that even the master martini makers themselves eventually turned that great responsibility over to her at the regular afternoon staff conferences.

Martinis, however, were not on the agenda when the telephone rang in Dr. Pierce's office at ten-thirty this bright morning. He was paying a rare (for him) tribute to a fellow practitioner of the healing arts to whom he referred as a "gas passer," but whom Student Nurse Miller knew was more formally known as an anesthesiologist. The gas passer on duty during this morning's jerking of the gall bladder had plied his trade well, in fact better than well, and when the telephone rang, Dr. Pierce was explaining to Student Nurse Miller just how valuable the gas passer's contribution had been.

"Grab that, sweetie, will you?" Hawkeye said, and

Student Nurse Miller snatched the phone before the first ring had finished.

"Office of the chief of surgery, Miss Miller speaking," she said; then, "One moment please." She covered the phone with her hand. "Some funny-talking broad says she's the international operator with a call for you from the Royal Hussidic Embassy in Paris. Is it for real? Or is it just Trapper John horsing around again?"

"Would to God that it were," Dr. Pierce said, taking the telephone. "Trapper John, at his most fiendish, isn't up to the Royal Hussidic Embassy in their innocence." He straightened his shoulders and took a deep breath.

"Dr. McIntyre," Dr. Pierce said. "I'm afraid Dr. Pierce is not available . . . oh. So it's you, Omar. How they hanging?"

At this point, solely because she considered it her nursely duty to keep herself fully apprised of any situation affecting the chief of surgery, and not in the least because of her female curiosity, Student Nurse Miller pushed the button that caused both ends of the conversation to be amplified through a speaker.

"Very comfortably, thank you, Doctor," the caller said, in British-accented English.

"I'm glad to hear that," Dr. Pierce said.

"In the absence of His Royal Highness, Doctor, I am charged with rendering every service at my disposal to His Excellency El Noil Snoil the Magnificent."

"Where's his nibs?" Hawkeye asked curiously.

"His Royal Highness is in San Francisco, Doctor, on an affair of state."

"What kind of affair of state? The kind you write down, or the other kind?"

"His Royal Highness has not seen fit to make me privy to his agenda, Doctor," Sheikh Abdullah said.

"Well, what's on your mind?"

"As I said, in the absence of His Royal Highness, I am charged with taking care of El Noil Snoil the Magnificent," Sheikh Abdullah said. "I am calling at his instruction, Doctor."

"I really am reluctant to say this," Hawkeye said. "But go on."

"His Excellency, his two gentlemen friends, and of course, Prince, departed Orly Field two minutes ago for the United States, Doctor. His Excellency asked me to tell you that he regretted not being able to call you himself before he left, but that he felt you would understand."

"Well, you just tell Old Bull Bellow that I understand completely, and that I'm sorry that I can't meet him in San Francisco," Hawkeye said.

"Oh, he's not going to San Francisco, Doctor. His Excellency is going to Spruce Harbor."

"Oh, no!"

"The young gentleman with him requires immediate surgery," Sheikh Abdullah said. "I am instructed by His Excellency to inform you to do whatever is necessary. Cost is no object. Send the bill to our Washington embassy."

"Wait a minute. What young gentleman?"

"The one with the Russian guitar," Sheikh Abdullah said.

"What's wrong with him?"

"I do not know the precise medical terminology, Doctor. When he was examined at the Maestro's apartment, there was no room for me in the Maestro's bedroom. I do recall what the Maestro said just afterward, however."

"And what was that?"

"I wrote it down," the sheikh said. "Here it is. Quote, 'My God, his insides are coming out!' Unquote."

"You don't happen to have this young man's name, do you?"

"Yes, Doctor, I do. His name is Pancho Hermanez."

"I thought you said he was a Russian guitar player?"

"He is."

"Well, Abdullah, thank you for calling," Hawkeye said.

"I am just doing my duty as Allah and His Royal Highness have given me the light to see that duty," Sheikh Abdullah said. "It wasn't really what I had in mind when I was a student at the Georgetown School of Foreign Service."

"Well, we all have our cross—in your case, scimitar —to bear, Omar."

"One more thing, Doctor," the sheikh said. "They're coming in the Royal Le Discorde. That should put them in the United States in three hours. But since the only place Le Discorde is permitted to land is on the salt flats in Utah, that will mean another five hours flying from Utah to Maine in a conventional aircraft."

"Got it," Hawkeye said. "That will give me time to make some arrangements. Thanks again for the warning, Omar. Give my regards to the little women."

He broke the connection with his finger.

"Women?" Student Nurse Miller asked. "As in more than one?"

"The sheikh is required to have at least two wives," Hawkeye explained. "As a gesture of his patriotism, he has four."

Student Nurse Miller's mouth opened, but there was no chance to pursue the matter further, for Dr. Pierce had told the operator to connect him with the hospital administrator, Mr. T. Alfred Crumley.

"Crumbum?" Dr. Pierce said. "I have some good news and some bad news. The bad news is that your old friend Boris Alexandrovich Korsky-Rimsakov will be with us shortly."

"Over my dead body!" Mr. Crumley replied.

"The bills have been guaranteed by the Royal Hussidic Embassy."

"As I've always said, Doctor, we must stand prepared to render whatever medical attention is required without regard to race, creed, color, national origin, or the personal, all-around gross and offensive personality of the patient."

"I would suggest that we take over the entire isolation ward," Dr. Pierce said. "But aside from that suggestion, I leave the whole thing in your hands, Crumbum."

"Once again, Doctor, that's Crum*ley*, Crum*ley*, Crum*ley!*"

"Gotcha."

"Is that revolting little prince coming, too?"

"Not as far as I know. The patient's name is Pancho Hermanez. The only thing I know about him is that he's a Russian guitar player whose insides are coming out."

"You mean that Boris Alexandrovich Korsky-Rimsakov is not at death's door?"

"Not as far as I know," Dr. Pierce said.

"Pity," Mr. Crumley said, and the connection broke.

Dr. Pierce replaced the telephone in its cradle, and turned to Student Nurse Miller.

"Sweetie," he said, "how do you feel about six-foot-five-inch men generally regarded by the gentle sex as handsome beyond words and utterly devastating?"

"I understand them," she said.

"You do?"

"The poor things have the same problems that I do," Barbara Ann said. "You have no idea what a drag it is to be—like Hot Lips and me, now, and Nurse Flanagan in her prime—nothing more than a sex object."

"If such a creature," Dr. Pierce went on, "should, you should excuse the expression, make a pass at you, could you handle it?"

"I'm sure that such a man would not make a pass at me, but—as painful as the memory is, Hawkeye—I've had a good deal of experience in turning away passes. Under the most difficult of circumstances. What are you leading up to, Hawkeye?"

"We are about to be blessed with a visit from Old Bull Bellow, also known as Boris Alexandrovich Korsky-Rimsakov. He may or may not be the world's greatest opera singer, but he is without doubt the loudest and largest," Hawkeye said. "One of his friends . . . I didn't get this too clearly . . . is either suffering from a terminal illness or a newly discovered social disease. In any event, Boris and his pal are about to come here."

112

"I've heard Hot Lips speak of him," Barbara Ann said. "Poor fellow."

"Poor fellow?" Hawkeye repeated incredulously.

"Forgive me for saying this, Hawkeye," Barbara Ann said. "But someone like you simply can't understand what it is to be a male version of Hot Lips and me."

"And I was just starting to like you!" Hawkeye said. He got up and headed for the door. "One more crack like that, sweetie, and it's back to one-for-the-boys-in-the-back-row for you!"

As he reached the door, Chief Nurse Flanagan, also in surgical greens, pulled it open from the corridor.

"I was just coming to get you, Doctor," she said. "We're about ready for you. It's time to scrub."

"That's not all it's time for," Hawkeye said. "Guess which six-foot-five 280-pound warbler's coming to dinner?"

"There's nothing wrong with Boris?" Nurse Flanagan hastily inquired.

"Not with him. One of his friends, however, has a certain unspecified delicate condition that requires our attention. A male friend, I hasten to add."

The telephone rang. Hawkeye was closest to it, and picked it up himself.

"Well, that figures," he said. "OK, Crumbum, thanks for calling." He hung up and turned to Barbara Ann Miller. "We at Spruce Harbor, unlike people at some medical establishments, do not normally extend a glad hand to potential customers. But in this case, and since I can't go myself, I think you had better change clothes, sweetie, and get in my car and go down to the airport. Dr. Grogarty's patient is about to arrive."

"You want *me* to meet him?"

"Right, and tell them I'll be with them just as soon as I can."

"But why me?" Barbara Ann asked.

"Because right now, sweetie," Hawkeye said, "about the only thing of value this hospital can offer him is a look at a good-looking blonde to take his mind off his troubles."

"Boston area control, Learjet Double-O Poppa," the gentleman occupying the copilot's seat of the trim little jet said into his microphone.

"Go ahead, Double-O Poppa," the Boston air controller replied.

"Double-O Poppa over the Cambridge Omni at three zero thousand. Request that you close out our instrument flight plan at this time."

"Roger, Double-O Poppa. What is your final destination?"

"Spruce Harbor International, Maine," the copilot said.

"Double-O Poppa, say again your aircraft type?"

"This is an F-Model Learjet aircraft."

"Double-O Poppa, are you aware that the main . . . and only . . . runway at Spruce Harbor International is dirt and only 4,800 feet long?"

"Affirmative," Double-O Poppa's copilot replied.

"You're going to try to put that Learjet down in that cow pasture?"

"Affirmative."

"Go with God, my son," Boston said. "Boston area control closes out Learjet Double-O Poppa at heading of zero one five true. Change to frequency 121.9 megahertz at this time."

"Understand 121.9 megahertz," the copilot said. "Thank you, Boston." He made the necessary adjustments on the radio control panel. "Spruce Harbor International," he then said. "Learjet Double-O Poppa."

"Go ahead, Double-O Poppa."

"That you, Wrong Way?"*

"That you, Radar?"

"How are you, Wrong Way?"

"Where are you, little buddy?"

---

* The founder, proprietor, and control-tower operator of Spruce Harbor International Airport, Spruce Harbor, Maine, was Mr. Michelangelo Guiseppi Verdi Napolitano, who, after a distinguished career as a PFC gunner-radio operator with the Eighth United States Air Force during World War II (every other gunner-radio operator who had completed seventy-five missions was at least a sergeant), returned to Spruce Harbor to found the Napolitano Truck Garden and Crop-Spraying Service.

"We just passed over Boston, airspeed 480, descending through two-zero thousand, and about to take up a heading of due north." The copilot turned to the pilot. "Turn a little to the left, Colonel," he suggested. "I always like to make my approach from the ocean."

"Roger, Wilco," the pilot said. "If I start screwing up, take it, will you, Radar? I haven't flown since I came home from Korea."

"You're doing fine, Colonel," Radar said. "Take it right down to the deck. I always like to buzz the clinic when I'm on final."

"You still there, Radar?" Spruce Harbor asked.

"We're here. We should be on the deck in about five minutes," J. Robespierre O'Reilly said. "We filed an in-flight advisory about thirty minutes ago, Wrong Way. Did you pass it to Hawkeye?"

"Yeah," Wrong Way replied. "And you should see who he sent to meet you."

"Who's that?"

"Stacked like a you-know-what, Radar," Wrong Way said. "Oh, she wants to know do you need an ambulance?"

"No."

"Your patient can walk?"

"Not only can he walk, he's flying," Radar replied. "OK, Colonel, there it is, straight ahead. That red barn-like thing. That's the Finest Kind Fish Market and Medical Center. Don't get any closer than twenty feet. They've got a high TV antenna that you can't see until you're right there."

"Roger, Wilco," Colonel Whiley said.

"Gee," Radar said. "You sound just like Errol Flynn in *Eagle Squadron!*"

Moving at close to five hundred miles per hour, the Learjet, perhaps two hundred feet off the white-capped ocean, faced in toward the rockbound coast of Maine, on which perched a red building.

Dr. Cornelius E. Sattyn-Whiley, who was, truth to tell, more than a little nervous on several accounts—not the least of which was that, taking into consideration that his father was both a very sick man and hadn't flown for twenty-five years, his piloting this airplane wasn't a very good idea—now had something else to trouble him.

The little red building perched on the rockbound coast they were approaching at five hundred miles per hour had a sign painted on the roof that said, "Finest Kind Fish Market and Medical Clinic."

Although distracting the attention of Mr. O'Reilly under the circumstances was obviously not such a good idea, curiosity got the better of him. "Is that what we've flown from San Francisco to go to? That converted barn, surrounded by lobster traps and a mountain of beer cans?"

"Right," Radar said. "But only because Aloysius Grogarty knows Hawkeye and Trapper John. Otherwise, you'd probably have to go to the Spruce Harbor Medical Center."

Dr. Sattyn-Whiley now steeled himself against a crash. When it never came, he finally opened his eyes again.

"OK, Colonel," Radar was saying. "Get the nose up a little and stand by for when I cut power and reverse thrust. I'm going to lower the flaps and the gear."

"Got it," Colonel Whiley said. Dr. Sattyn-Whiley was aware that his father was more excited—and visibly happier—then he had ever seen him before.

"Flaps down," Radar called. "Gear down!"

A runway was suddenly directly in front of them.

"Put her down as close to the threshold as you can, Colonel," Radar said. "There's only 4,800 feet."

The nose dipped to the ground, and, for a moment, Dr. Sattyn-Whiley was sure they were going to crash. But at the last split-second, his father pulled back ever so slightly on the wheel, and the plane seemed to bounce on a cushion of air and then sink through it slowly, so that there was only a slight bump when the wheels made contact.

"Hold onto your teeth!" Radar called. The engines suddenly roared with power, and Dr. Sattyn-Wiley felt himself thrown against his shoulder straps as the

Learjet decelerated; the jet-thrust had been applied in reverse.

The plane, however, continued to eat up the runway at an alarming speed.

"Brakes!" Radar called, and there was another horrifying hydraulic noise from the innards of the plane.

No more than twenty feet from Spruce Harbor International's control tower, the Learjet finally slid to a halt.

"Very good for your first time," Radar said professionally. Colonel Whiley looked at him with quiet pride, some gratitude, and a great deal of satisfaction.

"My wife didn't like me to fly," he said. "So I gave it up."

"You should have done what I did," Radar said.

"What was that?"

"I taught my pumpkin how to fly," Radar said.

"Madame Korsky-Rimsakov is a pilot?" Dr. Sattyn-Wiley asked incredulously.

"Well, she busted her Airline Transport Rating exam when she took it," Radar said. "But she's still got her multi-engine jet instrument ticket, and she's checked out in this, of course. And our friend Horsey said she can practice on her vacation on one of his 747's and then take another shot at the Airline Transport exam."

"I never thought of teaching Caroline to fly," the colonel said wistfully. And then he looked out the window. "Gee, that's really like old times," he said. "Looking out the cockpit window and seeing something like that!"

He referred, of course, to Miss Barbara Ann Miller, who stood beside Wrong Way Napolitano, waiting for the cabin door to open.

Dr. Sattyn-Whiley was aware that his father was looking at the best-looking female he'd seen in a very long time as a good-looking female, period. He himself was very much aware that the good-looking blonde was in nurses' whites. And that made him very painfully aware of what they were doing here.

117

Chapter Nine

At just about this time, another member of the healing profession, Francis Burns, M.D., and his wife and helpmate, Sweetie-Baby, were checking into the Mark Hopkins Hotel in San Francisco, California.

Dr. Burns was attired in a blackish suit and wore a black shirt and a reversed collar.

"I believe you have a reservation for Dr. and Mrs. Burns," he said to the desk clerk.

"Just a moment, Reverend," the desk clerk said.

"Just call me 'Doctor,' son," Burns said. "If you please."

"Of course, Doctor," the desk clerk said.

"What real meaning have earthly titles?" Burns inquired. "Our reward will come later . . . upstairs."

"I understand perfectly, Doctor," the desk clerk said. "Oh, here it is. A nice little suite, and I see that our vice-president for charitable affairs has authorized a fifty-percent discount."

"Only fifty-percent?" Frank Burns inquired.

"I don't believe that he realized you were a man of the cloth, too, Doctor, so there will be another twenty-percent discount."

"That's better," Frank Burns said. "God bless you, son."

"Is Mrs. Burns with you, Rev—Doctor?"

"Yes," Frank Burns said, nodding toward Sweetie-Baby, who was sort of hiding behind a potted palm, holding her purse in front of her face. "There she is, God bless her."

118

The desk clerk banged his little bell and a bellboy appeared to carry the luggage. Frank Burns did not speak to Sweetie-Baby Burns all the way up to their suite. There were times when she annoyed him, and when he didn't understand her at all, and this was one of these times. She was being unreasonable and annoying about his clerical collar.

It wasn't as if he wasn't *entitled* to wear the clerical collar. He was a duly licensed minister of the Universal Church of All Faiths, and had a certificate from the Universal Church of All Faiths & Job Printing Company to prove it, a certificate that had cost him ten whole dollars.

Under the circumstances—since he had, out of the goodness of his heart, given the Universal Church people the ten dollars—it was only right and fair that he take advantage of the twenty-percent discount the airlines gave the clergy. And if it made airline porters and bellboys feel good to refuse a tip from a clergyman, would it be the Christian thing for him to do to deny them that simple pleasure?

Once they were inside their nice little suite, Sweetie-Baby, her face flushed, fled into the bedroom. Frank was left alone with the bellboy.

"You with GILIAFCC, Inc., Rev?"

"Just call me 'Doctor,' son," Frank Burns said. "Odd that you should ask."

"Are you?"

"One of the reasons I am in your charming city is to re-establish a relationship with one of the GILIAFCC, Inc., clergypersons," Frank Burns said. "Would you be good enough, son, to give me directions to their place of worship?"

"Certainly," the bellboy said. "Any cab driver can tell you, of course, but if you're walking, just head down Market Street until you come to the neon sign."

"What neon sign?"

"It's a rather large one, Rever—Doctor. It says 'Welcome Sinner!' "

"I see."

"Under the words, there's the Reverend Mother

119

Emeritus, shooting the first arrow," the bellboy went on. "From there, just follow the arrows."

"I beg pardon?"

"Not *really* the Reverend Mother Emeritus, of course," the bellboy explained. "A sign of her. You can't miss it. It's four stories high, and it's in four colors."

"And the arrows?"

"The sign shows her shooting a bow and arrow. They flash on and off, so it looks like the arrow's in flight. You understand?"

"I think so."

"And then when you get close to the Temple, actually the First Missionary Church—you can't miss it."

"Why not?"

"There's a thirty-foot statue of the Blessed Brother Buck being welcomed into Heaven by Saint Peter and Saint Michelangelo."

"*Saint* Michelangelo?"

"The GILIAFCC, Inc., thinks of him that way," the bellboy said. "As one of their own, so to speak."

"And you think I could find the Reverend Mother Emeritus there?"

"Not today," the bellboy said. "Tomorrow you probably could."

"Why not today?"

"She's not there today," the bellboy said reasonably. "Thats why you couldn't find her there today."

"Where *could* I find her today?"

"New Orleans, probably," the bellboy said. "That's where she lives. But she's coming here tomorrow. Here, look in the paper." He handed him a newspaper. There was a story on the front page, beneath a formal portrait of the Reverend Mother Emeritus:

SAN FRANCISCO, CALIF. Police Commissioner Boulder J. Ohio today threatened "quick arrest and even speedier trials" for anyone misbehaving during either the arrival ceremonies for the Reverend Mother Emeritus M. H. W. Wilson of the

120

God Is Love in All Forms Christian Church, Inc., or during the annual triumphal Sinner's Procession tomorrow night.

"I have cancelled all leaves and off-days for the entire force," the commissioner said in an interview, "and extra security will be in force both at the airport and all along the procession route. I will not tolerate this year the scandalous behavior that has unfortunately occurred in the past."

The commissioner, as an example of the tight security he plans to enforce, said that only *bona fide* travelers, with tickets to prove it, will be admitted to the terminal building at San Francisco International Airport after 3:00 P.M. tomorrow afternoon. He also said his men in blue will be equipped not only with standard riot gear, but also with cameras to photograph those who throw bottles and other objects at members of the procession. The photographs will be used as evidence in court.

"In cooperation with the GILIAFCC, Inc., officials," the commissioner went on, "we will check the identity of anyone who wishes to march in the procession. Only *bona fide* members of the GILIAFCC, Inc., will be permitted to march or to enter the picnic grounds on the Embarcadero."

Sweetie-Baby Burns walked back into the room just as Frank finished reading this newspaper story.

"Good news, Sweetie-Baby," Frank Burns said to her. "The pressing business that brings me to San Francisco can be delayed until tomorrow."

"Oh?"

"And I will thus be able to go with you when you ride the cable cars," he said. Turning to the bellboy, he said, "Clergymen, I believe, ride for free?"

"No, Rever—Doctor. They have to pay just like everybody else."

"In that case," Frank Burns said, "we'll save the cable cars for tomorrow. This afternoon we can just wander around the streets, looking at the sights."

About an hour after this fascinating interchange of information took place, Police Commissioner Boulder J. Ohio sat at his desk in the picturesque police headquarters building with two problems on his hands, neither of which he quite knew how to deal with.

His wife had just been arrested as a "suspicious hippie," and try as he would not to, he had to agree with the arresting officer that he, too, would have found it suspicious if he had seen the commissioner's official limousine cruising slowly down Grant Avenue (one of the streets bordering Chinatown) with a scantily dressed young woman riding on top, alternately quoting Confucius and throwing handfuls of rice at passersby.

The second problem was more pressing, because the pressee was at that moment in his outer office, while his wife was, at least for the moment, safely out of the way in the Chinatown Precinct drunk tank.

The commissioner was quite sure that he knew what was on the mind of Mrs. C. Edward Sattyn-Whiley, and equally sure that she was going to give him the benefit of her thinking in her own inimitable manner. He had on his desk a copy of the same newspaper the bellboy had shown to Frank Burns. It was obvious to him that the story had come to Mrs. Sattyn-Whiley's attention, and that she was going to inquire of him what his reasons were for permitting the Reverend Mother Emeritus and her faithful flock to return to San Francisco at all.

From his past experience with Mrs. C. Edward Sattyn-Whiley, he knew that there was no point in bringing up such Constitutional things as freedom of religion, assembly, or speech. He had been accused of nitpicking before. The bottom line was that the Reverend Mother Emeritus was coming back to town, and Mrs. C. Edward Sattyn-Whiley disapproved.

The commissioner reached into the drawer of his large and highly polished desk and withdrew from it a small brown paper bag, through the top of which stuck the capped neck of a bottle of spiritous liquor. The commissioner took a healthy pull at the bottle, grimaced, shook his head, looked thoughtful, and then took another pull.

He then replaced the bottle in the drawer, sprayed his open mouth with some Booze-B-Gone—a patented, rather aptly named product—and, steeling himself for the ordeal, ordered his secretary to show Mrs. C. Edward Sattyn-Whiley in.

He walked from behind the desk toward the door as the door opened.

He winced when he saw that Mrs. Sattyn-Whiley was accompanied by her attorney, the dean of the San Francisco Bar, J. Merton Gabriel.

"Good afternoon, Mrs. Sattyn-Whiley," the commissioner said. "How good of you to come to see me!"

"You've been drinking again, Mr. Ohio," she said. "I can smell the Booze-B-Gone." And then she started to sniffle into her hankie. Somewhat confused at this reaction to his having had a little nip and been caught at it, the commissioner did what any politician does when confused—he smiled at the other party and shook hands.

"Good to see you, counselor," he said.

"We have a bad situation here, Commissioner," Mr. Gabriel said. "A bad situation."

"I'm sure that we, as reasonable people, can reach a reasonable resolution of our differences," the commissioner said.

Mrs. Sattyn-Whiley blew her nose, rather loudly, and then spoke.

"My husband, Commissioner, is missing," she said. "And I know who's responsible."

"I didn't know he even knew her," the commissioner said.

"Knew who?"

"The Reverend Mother Emeritus of the God Is Love in All Forms Christian Church, Inc.," the commissioner said. "Who else?"

"I was referring to that outrageous Irish charlatan, Aloysius J. Grogarty," she said. "How dare you suggest that my Edward knows that terrible woman?"

"Perhaps we had better start at the beginning, Mrs.

Sattyn-Whiley," the commissioner said. "I'm a little confused."

"That's not surprising," she said.

"May I offer you a cup of coffee?"

"I'd rather have some of whatever it is you simply reek of," she said. "My world has collapsed around me."

"You want some of my Booze-B-Gone?" the commissioner asked.

"I need something to steady my nerves," she said.

Somewhat hesitantly, the commissioner took the brown paper bag from his desk.

"That'll do," Mrs. Sattyn-Whiley said. She took it from him and took a healthy pull from the neck of the bottle.

The commissioner was now really worried. He would never have dreamed it possible that Mrs. C. Edward Sattyn-Whiley would take a healthy belt from the neck of a bottle in the privacy of her mansion, much less in his office.

"I come to you, Commissioner," Mrs. Sattyn-Whiley said, "a lonely and frightened woman with nowhere else to turn."

"Tell me what I can do, Mrs. Sattyn-Whiley," he said. "How may I be of assistance?"

"You can throw that Irish scalawag in jail," she said. "Quietly, of course. I wouldn't want this to get out."

"What is it, exactly, that you wouldn't want to get out?"

"Never underestimate the Irish, Commissioner," Mrs. Sattyn-Whiley said. "There is apparently no depth to which they will not sink to gain revenge!"

"I suppose that's so," the commissioner said. "Exactly what has Dr. Grogarty done, Mrs. Sattyn-Whiley?"

"He's kidnapped my Edward, that's what he's done!" she said. "And my son, too!"

"Let me see if I have this straight," the commissioner said. "Dr. Aloysius J. Grogarty, chief of staff of the Grogarty Clinic—that Grogarty?"

"That one!"

"Has kidnapped Colonel C. Edward Whiley and your son?"

"My son the doctor," she said. "Dr. Cornelius E. Sattyn-Whiley."

"And do you have any idea *why* Dr. Grogarty has kidnapped your son and husband?"

"You bet I do!" she said. "He's done it to make a laughing stock out of me before my friends."

"Would you mind explaining that?"

"You tell him, Merton," Mrs. Sattyn-Whiley said. "I don't have the strength." She uncorked the bottle and took another pull at it.

"It goes back to the days of World War II," J. Merton Gabriel said, "when Colonel Whiley, then Major, fell under the evil influence of Dr. Grogarty while in the service."

"Oh?"

"My Edward was nothing more than a boy—in fact, he was known as the Boy Major," Mrs. Sattyn-Whiley said. "And he was obviously naïve, impressionable, and vulnerable to that awful man's influence."

"I see."

"Major Whiley made the acquaintance of Dr. Grogarty, then a lieutenant of the medical corps, when he sought his professional services," the lawyer said.

"Was he ill?"

"He was under a great mental strain," J. Merton Gabriel said.

"You don't get to be a nineteen-year-old major with fifteen kills without undergoing a certain strain," Mrs. C. Edward Sattyn-Whiley said.

"I see. And he went to Dr. Grogarty for treatment?"

"And at his hands, received the first liquor that ever passed his innocent lips," Mrs. Sattyn-Whiley said. "That's what that charlatan prescribed for my little Eddie." She began to sniffle again.

"And when the war was over, and they came home, he insisted on maintaining the relationship. Can you imagine the effrontery of that shanty-Irish charlatan, that Barbary Coast ne'er-do-well, imagining that he

125

could remain friends with C. Edward Whiley, simply because he had saved his life during the war?"

"He saved his life? By giving him booze?"

"Eddie was shot down in the jungle behind enemy lines," Mrs. Sattyn-Whiley explained. "That awful Irisher parachuted into the jungle to set his broken leg. He and some sergeant then carried Eddie back through the lines to safety. But that's what doctors are for, aren't they?"

"I suppose you could look at it that way," the commissioner replied. "And you say he presumed on this casual wartime acquaintance when they both returned to San Francisco?"

"I can't prove it, of course," Mrs. Sattyn-Whiley said. "It was before we were married and I began to manage my poor little Eddie's affairs, but I have reason to believe that my poor little Eddie was cajoled into providing Grogarty with the money to start the Grogarty Clinic."

"I see."

"I told Eddie that I would not become his bride unless he shut off, once and for all, any connection with that awful man."

"And he, of course, did?"

"Not at first," she said, and blew her nose again. "At first, he told me to go to hell—he was still very much under his influence, you see. I was wise enough to see that, of course, and withdrew my objections until after we were married."

"I see."

"And do you know how that Irishman responded to my big-heartedness?"

"I have no idea."

"He and the sergeant from the jungle showed up at the wedding," she said. "Between them, they made indecent proposals to *five* of my bridesmaids."

"Shocking!" the commissioner said. "It was then that you were finally able to sever the relationship?"

"No, I am ashamed to say," Mrs. Sattyn-Whiley said. "I was blind with love at the time and let it pass. Besides, there were other considerations."

"Oh?"

"There's no accounting for tastes, you know," Mrs. Sattyn-Whiley replied. "Cynthia Forbes Robinson, one of my bridesmaids, eloped the day after my wedding."

"What's that got to do with it?"

"She eloped with the sergeant," she said. "At the time I thought she was mad. It was only years later that I found out he owned a 200,000-acre ranch and 375 oil wells in Texas. Under the circumstances, I thought it best to let things ride awhile."

"That's understandable."

"It was only when that awful man . . . I'm a lady and refuse to repeat what he said about me at Cornelius Dear's second birthday party—suffice it to say that Eddie was brought to his senses, and that man was thereafter banished from our lives."

"Forgive me, Mrs. Sattyn-Whiley, but I'm a police officer, and we deal with facts. What has all this to do with what you say is the kidnapping of your son and husband?"

"Grogarty did it!" she said. "It's as plain as the nose on your face, which is to say, very obvious, indeed."

"How is that?"

"Cornelius Dear has just returned home from college," Mrs. Sattyn-Whiley said. "Tomorrow night, I was going to re-present him to society at my home. I invited all the eligible young women of San Francisco—and their parents, of course."

"I still don't follow you."

"Grogarty, who has smarted all these years under his rejection by his betters, is going to ruin not only my party, but also Cornelius Dear's and my poor Eddie's reputations forever!"

"How's he going to do that?"

"He's going to deliver my poor little Eddie and Cornelius Dear to the party dead drunk!"

"Fiendish idea," the commissioner said. "But how do you know this?"

"He said so," she said. "Just two hours ago."

"He *told* you this?" the commissioner said. "I thought you didn't speak to him."

"I don't," she said. "I had J. Merton Gabriel call for me."

"I had spoken to Dr. Grogarty previously on this matter," the lawyer interjected.

"Why did Mr. Gabriel call him in the first place?" the commissioner asked Mrs. Sattyn-Whiley.

"Because my poor little Eddie and Cornelius Dear were seen leaving the opera with him, that's why!" she said. *"Madame Butterfly* had barely begun when Cornelius Dear was summoned from his seat in the belief that his medical skills were required. My poor Eddie was immediately suspicious, of course, and went after him. That's the last time I saw either of them."

"When they didn't return by the time *Madame Butterfly* was over," J. Merton Gabriel said, "Mrs. Sattyn-Whiley contacted me."

"Why didn't she contact the police?"

"I told you, we don't want this in the papers," Mrs. Sattyn-Whiley snapped.

"And all I could find out was that both had been seen leaving the building. Colonel Whiley was being supported by Dr. Grogarty, and at first, Dr. Grogarty would tell me nothing," J. Merton Gabriel said. "But two hours ago I telephoned Dr. Grogarty and ordered him to produce, instantly and forthwith, both of them."

"And what did Dr. Grogarty say?"

" 'Tell Caroline not to worry' is what he said," Mr. Gabriel replied. " 'With a little bit of luck, I'll have both of them back, dead drunk, in time for her party.' "

"That's all?"

" 'And tell her that I might just be with them, and just as drunk,' is what else he said," Gabriel concluded.

"So now you know why we're here," Mrs. Sattyn-Whiley said. "We want you to get them back for me as soon as possible . . . and as quietly as possible."

"Unfortunately, Mrs. Sattyn-Whiley," the commissioner began, "and as I'm sure Mr. Gabriel will tell you, both your husband and your son are over twenty-one. If they choose to get drunk with Dr. Grogarty, there's nothing, as much as I would like to help you, that the San Francisco Police Department can do about it."

Mrs. Sattyn-Whiley drew herself up to her full height.

"Commissioner," she said, pronouncing each syllable carefully, "I am prepared to pay any price, make any sacrifice, to have my husband and son restored—sober, of course—to me without any vulgar mention of their absence and return in the press."

"Precisely what are you saying, Mrs. Sattyn-Whiley?"

"I happen to know, Commissioner," Mrs. Sattyn-Whiley said, "that your mother, that sainted woman, as well as many other people of refinement, are distressed at your own choice of a wife."

"Loving Seagull *is* a little hard to understand until you get to know her," the commissioner admitted. "But how can you help me out with my mother?"

"You get my son and husband back to me, Commissioner, in the condition I described, and I personally will put your weird wife up for membership in the Opera Guild," she said. "That will certainly shut up even your sainted mother."

"Go home, Mrs. Sattyn-Whiley," the commissioner said, "and put this small little problem from your mind. Boulder J. Ohio himself will take personal charge."

He flipped the switch on his intercom.

"Get me Dr. Aloysius J. Grogarty on the line—immediately!" he snapped. Then he ushered Mrs. C. Edward Sattyn-Whiley and Mr. J. Merton Gabriel from his office.

As she left, Mrs. Sattyn-Whiley turned and smiled and offered a final word. "And if you don't, Commissioner, I wouldn't run for office—even for dogcatcher—again, if I were you."

It took fifteen minutes to get Dr. Aloysius J. Grogarty on the telephone.

"Sorry it took so long to get back to you, Ohio," Dr.

129

Grogarty said, "but I was busy looking out the window at the birds. What's on your mind?"

"I have a certain emergency matter of a delicate nature, Doctor," the commissioner began.

"Not another dose of cl—"

"Nothing like that, sir. This is a genuine emergency."

"Commissioner, I have nothing but the most profound respect for the San Francisco Police Department, those underpaid and overworked stalwart defenders of law and order, and I always place myself completely at their service whenever asked. You, Boulder J. Ohio, however, are nothing but one more lousy politician with his hand out, so get to the point —I'm a busy man."

As delicately as he could, Commissioner Ohio explained why it was important that Colonel Whiley and Dr. Sattyn-Whiley be instantly sobered up and quietly and immediately returned to the Sattyn-Whiley mansion.

"Mind your own business, Ohio," Dr. Grogarty said, and hung up.

The commissioner, of course, tried to call him back, to let him know that you just didn't hang up on the police commissioner. The Grogarty Clinic informed him that Dr. Grogarty had just left for Antarctica.

Commissioner Ohio then called in his senior staff, all career policemen, and told them they had a little, ha-ha, problem. Colonel C. Edward Wiley and Dr. Cornelius Sattyn-Whiley, celebrating the latter's return, had taken one or two too many.

"Put out an all-points bulletin," he ordered. "Find them! I don't care how you do it, but when you find them, take them to the Sattyn-Whiley mansion. In strait jackets if necessary." He had another thought. "And take whoever is with them with you."

He had a delightful mental picture of Dr. Aloysius J. Grogarty—he who had dared to hang up on him, the source of all the trouble—being delivered to the Sattyn-Whiley mansion in a strait jacket.

Chapter Ten

At just about this time in San Carlos, the sun-baked capital of San Sebastian, after months of careful planning, S-Second of M-Minute of H-Hour of D-Day arrived for the leaders of the legitimate government of San Sebastian, who had been thrown out of office when the government had, six months before, been overturned by the People's Democratic Fascist Republic.

With two-thirds of the nation's armored forces behind him, and three-quarters of the nation's air force in the skies overhead,* Colonel José Malinguez, leader of the junta, advanced on the Maximum Leader's (formerly President's) Palace, on horseback, and called for the unconditional surrender of the incumbents.

At first there was resistance—or, at least, no acknowledgement of his presence at all—but when Colonel Malinguez fired a round from his lead tank's

---

* The armored forces and the air force of San Sebastian consisted, respectively, of three M4A3 tanks (acquired from the United States Army as surplus in 1940) and four DeHavilland "Beaver" aircraft on floats. The single-engine, six-passenger silver birds, which had a top speed of just over 100 miles an hour, had also been acquired from the U.S. Army. They had been used by a mapping and topographic team of the Corps of Engineers, and had been abandoned in San Sebastian when the pilots, feeling then unsafe, had refused to even try to fly them any more, much less try to fly them all the way back to the States. There were also, of course, the San Sebastian Artillery (two French 75-mm cannons, which could be taken apart so they might be carried on mule-back) and the San Sebastian Infantry (150 men strong) armed with Swiss rifles acquired in 1890 when the Swiss converted to weapons utilizing smokeless powder.

cannon at the door of the palace (no damage occurred; the armored force had at its disposal only blank ammunition), the men who six months before had seized power came out with their hands raised high in surrender.

While members of the junta loaded their prisoners into trucks commandeered from the San Sebastian-American Jolly Jumbo Banana Company* for transport to the airport and exile from the country, Colonel Malinguez made his way to the basement of the President's Palace in search of the former President of the Republic, Señor El Presidente General Francisco Hermanez—who, it had been learned, had been held in durance vile since the revolution.

Señor El Presidente was located by following a dense blue cloud of cigar smoke to its source, a small cubicle in the far end of the basement.

"In here, my Colonel!" the officer with Colonel Malinguez said, as he raised the butt of his rifle and smashed at the door knob. The rifle stock snapped. As Colonel Malinguez and the officer stared at it with mute resignation, the door opened, and a rather portly gentleman, wearing riding breeches held up with suspenders and a sleeveless undershirt, peered out.

"It wasn't locked," he said.

"Señor El Presidente!" Colonel Malinguez cried. "The revolution has succeeded! You are free again!"

"Well, thanks for nothing, José," the chap in the sleeveless T-shirt and riding breeches said.

"You don't understand, El Presidente," the colonel went on.

"I understand perfectly," El Presidente replied. "But I've had a lot of time to think since I've been here in the basement. And I made up my mind, José, that I'm through begging. If we can't make it with the bananas, then to hell with it. Let the People's Democratic Fascist Republic worry about it. Where is he, anyway?"

---

* Except for semiannual sales of bat guano for approximately $26,500, the banana trade, which had the year before grossed $117,500, was San Sebastian's sole source of foreign exchange.

"Where is who, El Presidente?"

"Gus."

"Gus who?"

"Gus El Maximum Leader, that's who," El Presidente snapped.

"He has been exported to Costa Rica, El Presidente," the colonel said.

"How, on a bicycle?"

"By aircraft of the San Sebastian Air Force, El Presidente."

"And who's going to pay for the gas?"

"El Chancellor of the Exchequer, of course, El Presidente, who else?"

"And what's he going to use for money?"

"Swiss francs, El Presidente," the colonel replied.

"The only Swiss francs in the country, the last time I looked, were in the National Museum."

"We are about to solve our money problems, El Presidente," the colonel said. "Under your leadership, of course."

El Presidente looked at him with patient derision in his eyes. "You always were a little weird, José," he said. "I always said that. This country was bankrupt when my grandfather, may he rest in peace, took over. And things, money-wise, have gotten steadily worse since."

"There has been a new development, El Presidente," the colonel said. "One of which you, since you have been in durance vile for these past six months, could not possibly have heard about."

"The whole country has been repossessed?" El Presidente said. "I've been hoping for that. Then we're on welfare? Who repossessed us? What did they do, draw straws to see who got stuck with us?"

"If you will come with me, El Presidente?" the colonel said, making a gesture and a little bow toward the door.

"Where?" El Presidente asked suspiciously.

"To the San Sebastian Hilton," the colonel said. "Formerly the Democratic Fascist House of the People. And before that, of course, the San Sebastian Hilton."

"What are we going there for?" El Presidente asked. But even as he spoke, he slipped into his riding boots and pulled his tunic on.

Fifteen minutes later, after passing through downtown San Carlos through hordes of recently liberated San Sebastianites, who shouted and screamed and threw over-ripe bananas at the Presidential Jeep, the colonel and El Presidente arrived at the San Sebastian Hilton.

Colonel Malinguez led El Presidente into the cocktail lounge, where six gloriously uniformed men were gathered around an electronic Ping-Pong game.

"Colonel," Colonel Malinguez said to the next-to-largest of these men, whose uniform seemed to be an unholy marriage of that worn by the British Navy at the Battle of Trafalgar and that worn by doormen of better-class New York City high-rise condominiums, "I have the honor to present General Francisco Hermanez, recently liberated El Presidente of San Sebastian."

"Welcome back from the slammer, General," the man said. Instead of offering his hand, he offered a half-gallon bottle of Old White Stagg Blended Kentucky Bourbon. "Have a little snort," he said.

"Who is this man?" El Presidente inquired, somewhat haughtily, but taking the bottle nevertheless.

"Señor El Presidente, I have the honor to present Colonel Jean-Pierre de la Chevaux, Louisiana National Guard."

"So, the *Americans* repossessed us," El Presidente said. "I could ask for nothing more. How soon, Colonel, can we expect to start receiving foreign aid?"

"Colonel de la Chevaux—" Colonel Malinguez began.

"You can call me 'Horsey,' El Presidente," the man interrupted.

"—has a little business proposition for us," Colonel Malinguez finished.

"What kind of a business proposition?"

134

"The colonel is in the oil business, El Presidente," Colonel Malinguez said. He was facing away from Colonel de la Chevaux, so that Colonel de la Chevaux could not see him wink. "He believes that beneath the fertile ground of our beloved country are untold oil reserves."

El Presidente looked at Colonel Malinguez with new-found admiration. Perhaps he wasn't as stupid as he appeared. There was no oil whatever in San Sebastian. The entire country had been diligently searched half a dozen times, and there hadn't been enough oil to grease a Timex watch. And yet here was a Yankee, just about begging to be fleeced.

"And what is the nature of your proposition, Colonel?" El Presidente inquired, helping himself to another belt of the Old White Stagg.

"The standard proposition," Horsey de la Chevaux replied. "We'll give you a little earnest money. Then, completely at our expense, we'll look for oil. If we find oil, we'll take ten percent for our share. We'll pay all marketing expenses, of course."

"I see. You mentioned earnest money. What sort of figure did you have in mind? Just a rough figure, of course. In a business proposition of such magnitude, we could not come to a hasty conclusion, but we'll listen to your proposition."

"Well, I thought a couple of million for openers," Colonel de la Chevaux replied.

"You just made yourself a deal, Colonel," El Presidente said very quickly.

"Just to see where we stand," Horsey went on, "two million for the right to drill six holes on 160 acres I happened to smell . . . I mean see."

"At the current rate of exchange, Colonel," El Presidente said, "two million bananarios* would come to something around $2,500."

---

* The San Sebastian currency system is based on the bananario. There are 100 pennarinos to one bananario. The currency has been not listed on any foreign-exchange market since 1937, when it became apparent that no one was willing to exchange hard cash of any variety for bananarios, no matter how favorable the rate.

"I was talking about *dollars,* El Presidente," Horsey de la Chevaux said. "I'll give you two million dollars for drilling rights on the 160 acres I have in mind. You would give an option to drill more, once we get our feet wet."

It was El Presidente's considered opinion that all this Yankee was going to get with his six holes—for that matter, with holes drilled at 50-foot intervals from border to border—was wet feet (the topography of San Sebastian is essentially swamp), but he refrained from offering this observation.

"Two million *dollars? American* dollars?"

"Either that, or the same figure in Swiss francs, whichever you want," Horsey said.

"Colonel," El Presidente said, "I pride myself on being a judge of character. I can tell, by looking into your somewhat bloodshot eyes, that you are a man of your word. It will, I am sure, be a pleasure to do business with you."

"Fine," Colonel de la Chevaux said.

"How long will it take you to draw up the contracts?" El Presidente said. "And in the meantime, I don't suppose you could see your way clear to advance this country, simply as a gesture of your good intentions, a small advance. Say a thousand dollars? How about five hundred?"

"François," Horsey said to the largest man in his group, François Mulligan, who carried the money bags around. "Let me have a couple of million."

"Francs?" Mr. Mulligan inquired, as he unzipped a bag, "or deutsche marks or dollars?"

"If it's all the same to you, Colonel," El Presidente said, "how about some of each?"

"Whatever you say," Horsey said. "We'll just make it three million down. That way François won't have to try to divide two million by three."

Within a matter of moments, the currency had changed hands, and El Presidente had signed the necessary documents.

Then, overcome by emotion, he suddenly grabbed

Colonel de la Chevaux by the lapels and kissed him, wetly, on each cheek.

"Hey, watch it!" Horsey said. "Not only am I not like that, but you need a shave, El Presidente!"

"By the authority vested in me by the constitution of San Sebastian, written by my own grandfather, may he rest in peace, I name you a Commander of the Order of St. Sebastian, Third Class," El Presidente said.

"Gee, that's nice of you," Colonel de la Chevaux said as El Presidente snatched the medal of that order from the chest of Colonel Malinguez and pinned it on Horsey. Caught up in the emotion of the moment himself, Horsey snatched the Order of the Guardians of the Peace and Tranquility of the Knights of Columbus from François Mulligan's chest and pinned it onto El Presidente's tunic.

"By the authority vested in me as Grand Exalted Keeper of the Golden Fleece, Bayou Perdu Council, Knights of Columbus, I name you herewith an honorary member of the K. of C.," Horsey said. He did not, however, kiss El Presidente.

"When do you think you'll start looking for the oil, Colonel?" El Presidente said, examining the medal with pleasure. He had to admit it was more impressive than the one he had given Colonel de la Chevaux. He wondered if the diamonds were real.

"It'll take a little time," Colonel de la Chevaux replied. "I'll get on the radio and order a drilling rig flown here from New Orleans. With the expected delay, we won't start digging until, say, day after tomorrow."

"By then, regretfully, I will not be here."

"Where are you going, El Presidente?" Colonel Malinguez asked, at the same time putting one hand on the stack of bills on the table.

"Well, first things first," El Presidente said. "First, I will deposit this money in the national treasury. Then I will ask El Chancellor of the Exchequer for my six months' back pay. With what I have saved up, I should have enough money to buy a tourist-class

137

ticket to Paris so that I can see my beloved grandson, Pancho."

"Hell, El Presidente," Horsey de la Chevaux said. "I'm on my way to Abzug. Be no trouble at all to drop you off in Paris. The least I can do, after you gave me this pretty medal."

"I don't want to impose," El Presidente said.

"Not at all," Horsey said. He extended the bottle again. "Have another belt, El Presidente."

"Don't mind if I do," El Presidente said.

TOP PRIORITY
FROM UNITED STATES EMBASSY,
SAN JOSÉ, COSTA RICA
TO THE STATE DEPARTMENT, WASHINGTON
ATTENTION: BANANA REPUBLICS DESK

1. THE GOVERNMENT OF THE PEOPLE'S DEMOCRATIC FASCIST REPUBLIC OF SAN SEBASTIAN WAS OVERTHROWN TODAY IN A COUP D'ETAT LED BY COLONEL JOSÉ MALINGUEZ.

2. ACCORDING TO USUALLY RELIABLE SOURCES, THE COUP WAS, WITH THE EXCEPTION OF A PRIVATE FIRST CLASS SIMON SANCHEZ-GOMEZ, SR., WHO FELL OUT OF A JEEP AND GAVE HIS KNEE A NASTY CUT, BLOODLESS.

3. GUSTAV "BIG GUS" GONZALO, FORMER MAXIMUM LEADER, AND MEMBERS OF HIS IMMEDIATE STAFF, PLUS HIS FAMILY AND SEÑORITA ROSE LOPEZ, DESCRIBED AS HIS "GOOD FRIEND AND CONFIDANTE," WERE EXILED FROM THE COUNTRY AND FLOWN TO SAN JOSÉ, COSTA RICA, BY AIRCRAFT OF THE REPUBLIC OF SAN SEBASTIAN AIR FORCE.

4. GENERAL FRANCISCO HERMANEZ, WHO HAD BEEN PRESIDENT OF THE REPUBLIC PRIOR TO THE PEOPLE'S DEMOCRATIC FASCIST REPUBLIC COUP D'ETAT OF SIX MONTHS AGO, AND WHO HAD SINCE BEEN HELD PRISONER IN THE MAXIMUM LEADER'S (FORMERLY PRESIDENTE'S) PALACE EVER SINCE,

HAS BEEN RELEASED AND HAS RESUMED CONTROL OF THE GOVERNMENT.

5. FORMER MAXIMUM LEADER GONZALO, HOWEVER, IN A PRESS CONFERENCE HELD IMMEDIATELY UPON HIS ARRIVAL AT SAN JOSÉ (COSTA RICA) INTERNATIONAL AIRPORT, CHARGED THAT THE CIA WAS CLEARLY RESPONSIBLE FOR HIS BEING DEPOSED. AS PROOF, HE POINTED TO THE FACT THAT IMMEDIATELY UPON HIS RELEASE FROW PRISON, EL PRESIDENTE HERMANEZ WENT TO THE SAN SEBASTIAN HILTON, WHERE HE CONFERRED WITH A GROUP OF AMERICANS IDENTIFIED AS COLONEL J. P. DE LA CHEVAUX AND HIS STAFF.

6. THE CIA, WHICH HAS A LARGE FILE ON COLONEL (LOUISIANA NATIONAL GUARD) DE LA CHEVAUX, FLATLY DENIES ANY ASSOCIATION WITH HIM VIS A VIS RESTORING GENERAL HERMANEZ TO POWER.

7. THE CIA BELIEVES THAT EL PRESIDENTE MAY HAVE ENTERED INTO SOME SORT OF FINANCIAL ARRANGEMENTS WITH CHEVAUX, BUT EXACTLY WHAT KIND IS NOT AT ALL CLEAR. SINCE SAN SEBASTIAN HAS NO PETROLEUM (OR OTHER NATURAL RESOURCES OF ANY KIND), AND NO CURRENCY RESERVES WHATEVER, IT IS HARD TO IMAGINE WHAT EL PRESIDENTE IS EITHER SELLING TO OR BUYING FROM CHEVAUX. IT IS POSSIBLE, HOWEVER, THAT EL PRESIDENTE IS ATTEMPTING TO SELL THE WHOLE COUNTRY (OR AT LEAST PARTS OF IT) TO CHEVAUX—ALTHOUGH IT IS NOT AT ALL CLEAR WHY ANYONE, INCLUDING CHEVAUX, WOULD WANT IT.

8. WHILE THIS MESSAGE WAS BEING DRAFTED, REDRAFTED, EDITED, AND SUBMITTED FOR AMBASSADORIAL REVIEW, THIS EMBASSY WAS INFORMED, CONFIDENTIALLY, BY THE CIA THAT THEIR MAN IN SAN SEBASTIAN HAD REPORTED THAT EL PRESIDENTE HAD LEFT THE COUNTRY IN A 747 JUMBO-JET AIRCRAFT BEARING CHE-

VAUX PETROLEUM CORPORATION MARKINGS, DESTINATION UNKNOWN.

    SPIRES I. RONALD

    CHARGE D'AFFAIRES & PASSPORT OFFICER

This message, when it reached the State Department in our nation's capital, did not, truth to tell, cause much of a stir. For one thing, the Banana Republics Desk was having its annual picnic in the Lyndon B. Johnson Memorial Gardens on the banks of the Potomac, and only a very junior foreign-service officer had been left behind to answer the phone and collect the pay checks.

She was so junior, in fact, that she possessed only a "top-secret" security clearance, and the messenger who delivered the radio-teletype message, which was classified "very top-secret," at first refused to hand it over.

Once that had been resolved (the junior officer was given an interim "very top-secret" security clearance, good only until one of her superiors got back from the picnic, other problems arose. For one thing, she could not find San Sebastian, either on the map or on the labels of the file drawers. She had not, of course, been entrusted with the keys to the file *cabinets,* both because they contained "very top-secret" security information and because that was where the deputy assistant vice-chief of the Banana Republics Desk kept his gin.

But, although a newcomer, she had already begun to, as she put it, "learn the ropes." She had, in other words, already learned rule one for a bureaucrat: When presented with a paper you don't understand, mark it "for your information" and put it as surreptitiously as possible in your immediate superior's "in" basket.

This accomplished, the young foreign-service officer returned to her desk and resumed painting her fingernails, dreaming of the day when she would have enough seniority to go on picnics with the rest of the gang.

En route to Paris from San Carlos, San Sebastian, aboard Colonel Horsey de la Chevaux's 747, Horsey and General El Presidente Francisco Hermanez, recently restored President of San Sebastian, became close friends.

They had a good deal in common in addition to their fondness for Old White Stagg Blended Kentucky Bourbon. Both had been born into, and spent long years in, poverty. Both had, on occasion, awakened to find themselves behind bars.

But it was more than this that brought together the two who had, in their heart of hearts, at first thought of each other as "one more lousy gringo" and as "a banana-republic Mussolini," respectively. They were kindred souls, and it didn't take long for both of them to find this out.

When the general had boarded the 747, Horsey de la Chevaux couldn't have cared less about the general's grandson, who was all alone in Paris. But an hour after they had taken off—long before they had opened the second half-gallon of Old White Stagg—Horsey excused himself and quietly went to the cockpit, where he had the flight engineer send off a message:

FROM CHEVAUX PETROLEUM NUMBER ONE
EN ROUTE PARIS
TO GENERAL MANAGER
FRANCO-CHEVAUX PETROLEUM
118 AVENUE DE LA CHAMPS-ELYSÉES
PARIS

DO WHATEVER IS NECESSARY TO LOCATE AND DELIVER TO ORLY FIELD TO MEET THIS AIRCRAFT ONE PANCHO HERMANEZ, MALE SAN SEBASTIAN, AGED TWENTY-TWO YEARS, LAST KNOWN ADDRESS STUDENT HOSTEL, UNIVERSITY OF PARIS, BOULEVARD ST. MICHEL. IF NECESSARY, CONTACT ROYAL HUSSIDIC EMBASSY AND GET THEIR ASSISTANCE.
J. P. DE LA CHEVAUX
CHAIRMAN & CHIEF EXECUTIVE OFFICER

Normally, of course (for Chevaux Petroleum, International was actually just one big happy family), Horsey signed his radio messages "Horsey." He signed this one the way he did because he wanted Francisco's grandson found in time for him to be on hand when they got to Paris. From his own experience, Horsey knew that it was a heart-warming experience to have one's close family on hand when one was released from durance vile.

Three hours out, as the level of the second half-gallon of Old White Stagg had begun to drop alarmingly, General El Presidente Francisco Hermanez started to cry.

"Whassamatter?" Horsey asked, not very clearly.

"You're a good man, Horsey," General El Presidente said, draping an arm around Horsey. "And I have been somewhat less than honest with you."

"Don't let that bother you, Francisco," Horsey replied. "You're a pretty good guy yourself, and I haven't been exactly telling you the truth, either."

"You mean, you never actually spent six months in the New Orleans Parish Bastille?"

"That isn't exactly what I meant," Horsey said.

"A simple lie—I forgive you. What harm is there in saying you spent six months on the New Orleans Parish road gang when you haven't?"

"I *did* spend six months on the road gang," Horsey said. "I was number 87-32098. That's not what I meant."

"Whatever you did, or said," El Presidente said, the tears now coursing down his leathery, unshaven cheeks, "it is not as bad as what I have done to you— before I knew you, and realized what a good fellow you are, Horsey. . . ."

"What did you do to me?" Horsey inquired, his curiosity now aroused.

"I want you to understand, my friend, that if it were not for the absolutely beyond-rehabilitation state of the San Sebastian economy . . ."

"Whassat mean?"

"If San Sebastian wasn't so broke," El Presidente explained, "if there had been any other way . . ."

"If you're going to make a confession," Horsey said, "get to the point."

"There is absolutely *no oil* in San Sebastian!" El Presidente said.

"Thass what you think," Horsey replied.

"That's what I *know*," El Presidente said. "Every major oil company in the world but yours has explored San Sebastian for oil," El Presidente said. "From border to border, from sea to shining sea."

"So what?" Horsey said, and he handed El Presidente the jug.

"They didn't find enough oil to grease a door knob," El Presidente confessed, taking a little pull.

"Don't worry about it," Horsey said.

"But I *knew* this, my friend," El Presidente said, taking another pull at the jug and then looking into Horsey's eyes, "when I signed the contract and took that money."

"Put it from your mind," Horsey said. "There's a lot more where that came from."

"You don't mind losing three million dollars? Being cheated out of three million dollars? *American* dollars?"

"Who's going to lose three million?" Horsey asked mysteriously.

"But I told you there's no oil in San Sebastian," El Presidente said.

"An *I* tol' *you*, Francisco, thass what *you* think," Horsey said, and he patted El Presidente consolingly on the back.

"I don't follow you, my friend," El Presidente replied in some confusion.

"You know what's the difference between Chevaux Petroleum and, say, Mobil? Or between Chevaux Petroleum and, say, Gulf?" Horsey asked.

"I don't quite follow you," El Presidente said.

Horsey put his finger to his nose (and made it on the third try). "Thass the difference, my friend!" he said with quiet pride.

"I beg your pardon?"

"Mobil's got geologists and engineers, all sorts of

highly paid people," Horsey said. "And so does Gulf. But what does Chevaux Petroleum have that Gulf and Mobil don't have?" It was a rhetorical question, to which he expected no answer, and which, indeed, he answered himself. On the fourth try, he managed to again connect his index finger with his nose. "It's a l'il secret," he said. "But I'm sure I can trust you."

"After the way I cheated you, how can you trust me?"

"Let me lay a little philosophy on you, Francisco," Horsey said. "You can't cheat an honest man. Especially an honest man with a nose like mine."

"With a nose like yours?"

"Ssssh!" Horsey said, swaying slightly and moving his finger from his nose to his mouth in the well-known gesture of secrecy. "Thass my secret!"

"Your nose is your secret?"

"You got it, Francisco!" Horsey said. "But don't tell anyone."

"I'm a little confused," El Presidente confessed.

"You're a little plastered, thass what's the matter with you," Horsey cried gaily. "That Old White Stagg'll sneak up and kick you, if you don't watch out!"

"What about your nose?"

"I smell with it," Horsey said triumphantly.

"Oh?"

"Oil, I mean," Horsey explained. "All I do is take a good whiff, and I know, right then and there, whether or not there's any oil."

"You do?"

"I had a little trouble in San Sebastian," Horsey said. "If you'll promise not to take offense, I'll admit it."

"Why should I take offense?"

"Well, between the smell of all that *Cheiroptera vespertilionodae* fecal matter* and all those rotten bananas, I had a hell of a time sniffing the oil."

---

* Colonel de la Chevaux here actually used the vernacular names for the mouse-like quadruped *Cheiroptera vespertilionodae* and for its droppings, but this is, after all, a high-toned book, and the editors felt that the vernacular noun, no matter how precise, might unnecessarily offend some readers.

"I am sorry that the smell offended you," El Presidente said, somewhat huffily, "but that bat do-do and the bananas are San Sebastian's only exports."

"I didn't say it *offended* me, Francisco," Horsey said. "Hell, wait till you smell Bayou Perdu. What I said was that I had to get *used* to it before I could sniff where the oil is."

"You're telling me that you can *smell* oil?" El Presidente said disbelievingly.

"What I'm telling you is that I *did* smell oil," Horsey said. "I was not being exactly truthful with you when I said I wanted to explore for oil, Francisco, old buddy. I knew that there was oil there."

"I find this hard to believe!" El Presidente said.

Horsey picked up the radio telephone.

"Hey, are we patched in to San Carlos yet?" he asked.

"Chevaux Petroleum, San Sebastian," a voice came back.

"Horsey here," Colonel de la Chevaux said. "How we doing?"

"Got a little problem, Horsey," the voice replied.

"What's that?"

"Well, as soon as we got here, I went out to the swamp where you drove the stake to tell us where to drill."

"And?"

"I run over the stake, Horsey."

"So?"

"Well, first it made a little hissing noise. And then it blew. Turned the Jeep over on its back. It's flowing ten thousand barrels a day it looks like, good heavy sweet crude. Lost the Jeep, though, Horsey. There's sort of a lake of oil out there, and I don't know where it sank."

"Well, make sure it don't catch on fire," Horsey said.

"What did that mean?" El Presidente asked.

"It means that Chevaux–San Sebastian Number One came in at about three feet," Horsey said. "Flowing ten thousand barrels a day. Seven dollars and twenty-

145

one cents a barrel, less our ten percent—that's about $68,500 a day for your government, Francisco."

General El Presidente Francisco Hermanez wrapped Colonel de la Chevaux in his arms and kissed him on both cheeks.

"It's a good thing I know you're a concerned grandfather," Horsey replied, blushing a little, "Let's have a little snort to celebrate. A ten-thousand-barrel-a-day well ain't much, but it's a start."

Chapter Eleven

"I'm Hawkeye Pierce," Hawkeye said, entering his office. "Sorry to have kept you waiting, but I had a little trouble jerking a kidney, and then, of course, I had to shower and dress." He was wearing a sweat shirt with a drawing of Ludwig von Beethoven on it and a pair of well-worn khaki pants. "I've always thought that it is very important to make a good first impression on a potential patient."

"Charley Whiley, Doctor," Colonel C. Edward Whiley said. "And this is my son, Cornie—Cornelius. *Dr.* Sattyn-Whiley."

Trapper John came into the office, trailed by Esther Flanagan. She was in crisp whites, and Trapper John was wearing a blue-and-white polka-dot jump suit.

"I would like to apologize, sir, for the shameful appearance of my colleague," he said. "I'm Trapper John McIntyre."

"I would like to express my appreciation for your letting me come here like this," Colonel Whiley said. "And let's clear the air by saying I've known Aloysius Grogarty long enough and well enough to know when he's clutching at straws."

"I'm Dr. Sattyn-Whiley, Doctor," Dr. Sattyn-Whiley said to Trapper John.

"We're glad to have you here with us," Trapper John said. "We have something very important for you to do."

"Yes, sir?" Dr. Sattyn-Whiley said eagerly.

"Nurse Flanagan?" Hawkeye said.

"Right away, Doctor," Nurse Flanagan said. She went to the bookcase, slid back a panel of phony books that concealed a refrigerator, and took from it a small plastic cooler. She placed this in Dr. Sattyn-Whiley's hands. He opened it.

"It's a six-pack of beer!"

"How perceptive our young doctors are getting to be," Hawkeye said.

"Over the next three hours," Trapper John said, "you are to administer at least two and no more than three of these to Student Nurse Barbara Ann Miller while you take a long walk along our picturesque mud flats with her. The other three are for you."

"I'd rather stay here, if you don't mind," Dr. Sattyn-Whiley said.

"And we'd rather you didn't," Hawkeye said. "We'll clue you in on what we find when you get back, but I don't want you breathing in my ear while we examine your father, got it?"

"Get out of here, Cornie," Colonel Whiley said. He waited until his son and Barbara Ann Miller had left.

"That's a good-looking female," he said. "She looks familiar, somehow." There was no reply to this. "Well, what happens now?"

Nurse Flanagan handed him a glass of clear liquid. "Drink this," she ordered. He tossed it down.

"What was that? Something for x-rays?"

"As a matter of fact, it was a martini," Trapper John said.

"Very light on the vermouth and without a vegetable salad," Hawkeye added. "I'd like to have you as relaxed as possible."

"In that case, I'll have another," Colonel Whiley said.

"When we finish," Hawkeye said.

"Isn't this sort of a waste of time and effort?" Colonel Whiley asked. "Why bother?"

"I have known Aloysius J. Grogarty long enough and well enough," Hawkeye said, "to do what he tells me to do."

"Touché," Colonel Whiley said.

"We're going to run another electrocardiogram and take a bunch of x-rays," Trapper John said. "And since you confess to being a friend of Grogarty's, we're going to give you a blood test."

Colonel Whiley chuckled.

"Let's take a walk down the corridor," Hawkeye said, "and give the patients' visitors something to talk about."

Radar O'Reilly was waiting in the corridor outside.

"Radar! Just the man I wanted to see," Hawkeye said.

"Is there something I can do?"

"In exactly one hour I want you to get in the swamp buggy and run it along the beach," Hawkeye said. "Do so until you find the young doctor and Student Nurse Miller."

"And?"

"If they should happen to be holding hands," Hawkeye said, "or looking as if they would like to be holding hands, then you just keep driving. If, however, they are acting like total strangers, then pick them up and take them over to the Bide-a-While. Tell Stanley I said to give him some of that genuine Polish vodka."*

When Radar had gone, Colonel Whiley said, "I had the same feeling about those two. And what a relief!"

"I beg your pardon?" Nurse Flanagan said.

"Cornie's never shown much interest in girls," the colonel said. "I was beginning to get a little worried."

"Barbara Ann Miller," Nurse Flanagan said, "is a very nice girl. I'm sure he sensed that."

"I have the strangest feeling I've seen her somewhere before," the colonel said. "I don't suppose there's any chance she's from San Francisco?"

"Well," Hawkeye said, "here we are at the x-ray room!"

An hour later there was a bulletin from Radar.

"Where are you?" Hawkeye asked.

"At the Bide-a-While," Radar replied.

"Oh, there was no magic, huh?" Hawkeye said, obviously disappointed.

---

* Dr. Pierce here made reference to the Bide-a-While Pool Hall / Ladies Served Fresh Lobsters & Clams Daily Restaurant and Saloon, Inc., and Stanley K. Warczinski, its proprietor.

"That's what I called about, Hawkeye," Radar said. "You didn't say anything about crying."

"What do you mean?"

"When I drove past in the beach buggy, they were sitting in a beached rowboat, hanging on to each other for all they were worth, the both of them crying."

"So you brought them to the Bide-a-While?"

"No," Radar said. "I figured the best thing to do was leave them be. I came here to keep an eye on them. You know, with that dime-in-the-slot telescope the guys use to watch the nudists?"

"You did the right thing, Radar," Hawkeye said. "Stay right where you are. We'll be in touch."

And two hours after that, Hawkeye telephoned Radar and told him to get in the swamp buggy and bring Dr. Sattyn-Whiley and Student Nurse Barbara Ann Miller to the hospital.

"Can you see them, Radar? They still sitting in the beached rowboat?"

"No."

"You mean you can't see them? Where did they go?"

"You asked if they were still sitting in the rowboat," Radar said. "They aren't sitting in the rowboat, Hawkeye."

"Well, then," Hawkeye said, "be sure you make a lot of noise when you drive up, Radar. Clash the gears, or blow the horns. Sing, if necessary."

"Gotcha," Radar said, and he hung up.

Twenty minutes later, Dr. Cornelius E. Sattyn-Whiley and Miss Barbara Ann Miller walked into Dr. Pierce's office to find Colonel Whiley, Nurse Flanagan, and Doctors Pierce and McIntyre waiting for them.

Mr. Whiley was attired in a striped terrycloth bathrobe, across the back of which was stitched the legend, "Matthew Q. Framingham Foundation Whist & Pinochle Team." He held in his hand what looked very much like, and what indeed was, a double martini.

They were holding hands. All of a sudden, they both seemed to suddenly, and simultaneously, become aware of this. Their hands separated as if they had been shocked.

"And how did you find our picturesque mud flats, Doctor?" Hawkeye said.

"Just beautiful!" Dr. Sattyn-Whiley said. "Gorgeous!"

"I think I'd better go," Barbara Ann Miller said. Her face was flushed. Dr. Sattyn-Whiley's face was pained.

"If it's all the same to you, Hawkeye," Colonel Whiley said, "let her stay."

"It's your party, Colonel," Hawkeye said.

"Is that what it is?" Dr. Sattyn-Whiley asked. "Then that is a martini in your hand?"

"That's a martini, all right, but you don't get one," Trapper John said.

"Why not?"

"For the same reason that Hawkeye, Nurse Flanagan, and I are standing here with our tongues hanging out," Trapper John said.

"Because we have just decided that tomorrow morning at the ungodly hour of 6 A.M., we are going to put on our green suits and cut a hole in your father," Hawkeye said.

"You've decided his condition is operable?" Dr. Sattyn-Whiley asked.

"That's a little too optimistic, Cornie," Colonel Whiley said. "What they have decided is that it's an operation, or, in Hawkeye's quaint little phrase, a one-way trip to the marble orchard."

"The x-rays are on the machine," Hawkeye said. "Have a look. And take a good look at the EKG, too."

Dr. Sattyn-Whiley went to the illuminated board on which half a dozen large x-ray films were displayed. There were four or five times that many others in manila envelopes on the table in front of the display apparatus.

"Did I understand that correctly? Am I to be permitted to assist?"

"You're going to be permitted to be in the operating room," Hawkeye said, "against my better judgment. But, as the colonel pointed out, unless we play the game his way, he's going to take his body and go home."

"Your mother, Cornie," the colonel said, "is going to raise hell about this no matter how it goes. If it goes the wrong way, I know she's going to try to blame Hawkeye and Trapper John. The reason I want you there is so that she'll have to push past you on her way to see her lawyer."

"All right," Dr. Sattyn-Whiley said. "Now what happens?"

"Well," Trapper John said, "as soon as you finish looking at the test results, Barbara Ann's going to take you to meet our gas passer. You'll assist him, and you'll have your hands full. He'll tell you what he expects of you, and when that's over, Nurse Flanagan has something she wants you to do for her."

"What's that?"

"She wants you to walk her dog," Trapper John said.

"I beg your pardon?"

"Three'll get you five, Doctor," Hawkeye said, "that if you found our mud flats beautiful and gorgeous by daylight, you've come to the conclusion that, presuming Barbara Ann was with you, they would really be something to see by moonlight."

Both Dr. Sattyn-Whiley and Student Nurse Miller looked slightly uncomfortable.

"And when one of my girls goes out on the mud flats in the moonlight," Nurse Flanagan said, "Princess goes along."

"Do I get another one of these?" Colonel Whiley asked.

"One more, Colonel," Trapper John said. "And then it's beddy-bye time for you."

"Miss Miller," Colonel Whiley asked, "may I ask you a personal question?"

"Certainly," Barbara Ann Miller answered.

"Have you ever been in San Francisco? Say about eighteen months ago?"

Barbara Ann Miller turned red, but she met his eyes and nodded her head.

"I thought so," the colonel said with satisfaction. "It's very nice to see you again."

"What's all that about?" Dr. Sattyn-Whiley said.

"When you get right down to it, Cornie," Colonel Whiley said, "it's none of your business, unless Miss Miller chooses to make it your business."

"I don't quite understand," Dr. Sattyn-Whiley said.

"That runs in the family," Colonel Whiley said. "We don't understand things—important things—until it's too late."

He took the martini Nurse Flanagan handed him and then started for the door.

"Will you all excuse me?" he said. "It's been a trying day, and I have a very important appointment in the morning." Then he turned and went to his son. He gave him a hug and then looked at Barbara Ann Miller.

"We fighter pilots in the olden days of World War II used to have a custom," he said. "We tried to kiss every pretty girl we saw. Especially when the pretty girl was so obviously a very nice girl." He then leaned forward and kissed Barbara Ann Miller on the forehead.

"Thank you," he said formally, and then he walked out of Hawkeye's office.

At half past five the next morning, Dr. Benjamin Pierce, wearing what his wife would have described as "a fresh pair of dirty, rotten khaki pants" and a turtleneck sweater, walked down the quiet corridors of the Spruce Harbor Medical Center toward the room assigned to Colonel C. Edward Whiley.

He found Dr. Trapper John McIntyre, Chief of Nursing Services Esther Flanagan, Student Nurse Barbara Ann Miller, and Dr. Cornelius E. Sattyn-Whiley (the last two holding hands, the others sipping at plastic cups of coffee) clustered around the door.

"What's up?" Hawkeye asked.

Trapper John pointed at the door. Scotch-taped to it was a note. It read: "Please do not disturb until necessary. Charley Whiley."

Hawkeye looked at his watch.

"It's now necessary," he said. As he pushed open the door, Nurse Flanagan picked up the preoperative-procedure medication Colonel Whiley would be given.

There was no one in the bed. And the door to the toilet was open, showing it empty. The window opening onto the parking lot was also open.

"Over here, Hawkeye," Nurse Flanagan said. There were two envelopes Scotch-taped to the mirror. One was addressed to Hawkeye and one to Dr. Sattyn-Whiley.

Hawkeye ripped them from the mirror, threw Dr. Sattyn-Whiley's to him, and tore open the envelope addressed to him. It read:

> Dear Hawkeye,
> Nothing personal, of course, but I think I would rather be cut by Aloysius Grogarty. If you think it can be done, then I can get him to do it. This is less a reflection on your skill and Trapper John's than it is the realization that if it goes the wrong way, Aloysius Grogarty, who has had thirty years' experience dealing with Caroline, can handle her better than you can.
> Would you please telephone him to let him know I'm coming? Presuming I make it all right, I think I would rather go directly from the airfield to the operating room, before I lose my nerve.
> And please tell Radar that for legal reasons, he had better tell the authorities that someone has stolen his airplane, for that's just what I'm about to do. Caroline kept me from flying for twenty-five years, and I figure that I'm entitled to one more flight, and stealing his airplane seemed to be the easiest way to do that. And just possibly the easiest way out of this mess.
> Faithfully,
> C. Edward Whiley.

Trapper John read the letter over Hawkeye's shoulder, and when Hawkeye was through, he handed the letter to Dr. Sattyn-Whiley. Wordlessly, Dr. Sattyn-Whiley handed his letter to Hawkeye. It read:

154

Dear Cornie,

One of the reasons I ducked out of the grand opening here is that I didn't want your first job to be a failure. Practice, they say, makes perfect, and you haven't had much time to practice.

For what it's worth, I like your Barbara Ann very much. I won't offer any advice on how to handle the situation, because you're a big boy now, but I will say this: Do what your heart tells you.

Love,
Dad.

Hawkeye handed the letter back to Dr. Sattyn-Whiley and reached for the telephone. "Get me Wrong Way Napolitano!" he said.

In a moment Wrong Way came on the line.

"Don't ask any questions, Wrong Way," he said. "Just keep anybody from taking off in Radar's airplane. I'm on my way out there."

He hung up and ran out of the room. The others followed him. He jumped into his car and raced toward the airport. The others jumped into other cars and followed him.

As they reached the airport, they heard the sound of engines. And as they turned onto the road that ran parallel to the runway, F-Model Learjet Double-O Poppa came down said runway, going in the opposite direction. As it reached them, it became airborne, and they saw the wheels retract as the plane gained altitude.

Hawkeye raced to the control tower, climbed the ladder, and accosted Wrong Way.

"I thought I told you to stop that airplane!"

"I tried," Wrong Way said. "I even lay down on the runway in front of him."

"So how come he's gone?"

"He just taxied around me," Wrong Way said. "I just got here myself. I was about to try and get him on the radio."

"Well, get him!" Hawkeye said.

155

"Double-O Poppa, this is Spruce Harbor," Wrong Way said into the microphone.

"Spruce Harbor, Double-O Poppa," Colonel Whiley's voice came back instantly. "Arrivederci, Wrong Way. Double-O Poppa out."

"He drunk, or what?" Wrong Way asked.

"I wish that's all it was," Hawkeye said.

"My God, here he comes back!" Wrong Way said. Double-O Poppa had taken off out to sea. Now it was coming back toward the airfield. It was no more than two hundred feet off the ground.

"My God!" Wrong Way said. "He's lost control!"

Hawkeye looked on with horror as the plane dipped one wing very low. But Double-O Poppa wasn't out of control. Double-O Poppa was executing a maneuver known as a roll. Colonel Whiley rolled the plane down the length of the field, straightened out, and disappeared, at a very low level, over the horizon, heading due west.

"That wasn't bad," Wrong Way said, making professional judgement.

Hawkeye picked up the telephone.

"Get me Dr. Aloysius J. Grogarty at the Grogarty Clinic in San Francisco," he said. "You'd better tell the operator that Hawkeye is calling, and we've got trouble."

"Spruce Harbor," the radio said, coming to life. "Air Hussid Eleven."

"Go ahead, Air Hussid Eleven," Wrong Way said. "But the answer, before you ask, is no. You can't put a Le Discorde in here."

"Air Hussid Eleven is a Sabreliner aircraft," the radio responded.

"Go away, Air Hussid, whatever you are, we got problems."

"Wrong Way, that you?" a fresh voice came on the radio.

"Yeah, Boris, it's me," Wrong Way said.

"Get on the telephone and tell Hawkeye that I am here, so that he may make the necessary arrangements," Boris Alexandrovich Korsky-Rimsakov said.

"Tell him," Hawkeye said, "that he's diverted to Nome, Alaska. The last thing I need right now is Boris!"

"Air Hussid Eleven, this is Spruce Harbor. You are diverted to Nome, Alaska," Wrong Way dutifully repeated.

"You have, for a spaghetti-eater, a rather interesting sense of humor," Boris replied. "We should be there in just a few minutes, Wrong Way."

"This better be important, Hawkeye," Dr. Aloysius J. Grogarty said, coming on the telephone. "Do you know what time it is out here?"

"Doctor," Hawkeye said. "'Colonel Whiley just took off from here, alone, in Radar's airplane, for San Francisco."

"Why did you let him do that?"

"I didn't *let* him," Hawkeye said. "It was his own idea. I told him I'd do the operation, and it was scheduled for six this morning. He ran away from the hospital and left a note saying that if he was to be cut, you'd have to do it."

"Well, he wasted his time, if that's what he's coming here for," Grogarty said. "I hate to pay you a compliment, Hawkeye, especially at this time of the morning, but the real reason I sent him to you was because I knew what he needed and knew that I couldn't do it. And I knew that you could."

"So what do we do now?"

"Do you know where he's *coming* out here?"

"To the airport, I suppose," Hawkeye replied. "Since he's flying."

"Well, I'll meet him at the airport," Dr. Grogarty said. "And I'll get him in my hospital. I'll keep him in my hospital—we're better at that sort of thing than you apparently are—until you get here."

"How am I supposed to get out there?"

"You're a bright boy, Hawkeye," Dr. Grogarty said. "You'll think of something." The line went dead. The radio came to life again.

"Spruce Harbor, Air Hussid Eleven over the outer marker and turning on final."

157

Chapter Twelve

Eventually, of course, the staff of the Banana Republics Desk of the State Department did return from their picnic at the Lyndon B. Johnson Memorial Gardens, and eventually the cable from San José regarding the events which had taken place in San Carlos, San Sebastian, came to the attention of the proper people.

By the time this happened, however, a second cable had been added to the first:

TOP PRIORITY
FROM UNITED STATES EMBASSY,
SAN JOSÉ, COSTA RICA
TO THE STATE DEPARTMENT, WASHINGTON
ATTENTION: BANANA REPUBLICS DESK

1. THE CIA's MAN IN SAN SEBASTIAN RE-PORTS CONFIDENTIALLY THAT HE HAS SOME REASON TO BELIEVE THAT OIL, AT LEAST IN SMALL QUANTITIES, HAS BEEN DISCOVERED IN SAN SEBASTIAN. HE BASES THIS BELIEF ON THE FOLLOWING:

    A. THERE IS A NEW LAKE IN THE SAN CAR-LOS SWAMP, THE LIQUID IN WHICH IS BROWN AND STICKY.

    B. EMPLOYEES OF THE SAN SEBASTIAN CHEVAUX PETROLEUM COMPANY HAVE BEEN ERECTING "NO SMOKING" SIGNS AROUND THE LAKE MENTIONED ABOVE.

C. The CIA has intercepted messages from the San Sebastian Chevaux Petroleum people to Chevaux Petroleum, New Orleans, that ordered emergency air shipment of oil tanks, pipelines, and other equipment normally used for the storage and shipment of oil; ordered the diversion at sea of the jumbo-tanker S.S. Hot Lips, en route to the Persian Gulf, to San Sebastian to pick up quote 250 thousand tons of heavy-gravity sweet crude unquote; and ordered a cable transfer to the account of the Government of San Sebastian of sixty-two million five hundred thousand dollars as an interim advance royalty payment.

2. While stating that none of the above should be considered conclusive proof that oil has been found in San Sebastian, the CIA feels that this remote possibility should be considered.

3. Inquiries to the Government of San Sebastian vis a vis the above have been met with the comment that only El Presidente can speak for the Government of San Sebastian. El Presidente, as previously advised, has left the country, apparently bound for France, in Colonel J. P. de la Chevaux's 747 aircraft.

4. Please advise.

SPIRES I. RONALD
CHARGE D'AFFAIRES & PASSPORT OFFICER

This cable, of course, was also eventually brought to the attention of the proper people, and this resulted in a third cable:

FROM DEPARTMENT OF STATE,
CHIEF DEPUTY ASSISTANT UNDER-SECRETARY FOR PETROLEUM AFFAIRS
TO UNITED STATES EMBASSY, PARIS, FRANCE

1.   REFERENCE IS MADE TO THE TWO TELETYPE MESSAGES FROM U.S. EMBASSY, SAN JOSÉ, COSTA RICA, TO STATE DEPARTMENT (REPEATED HEREWITH).

2.   BY DIRECTION OF THE SECRETARY OF STATE HIMSELF, THE U.S. AMBASSADOR TO FRANCE WILL MEET THE AIRCRAFT CARRYING HIS EXCELLENCY GENERAL EL PRESIDENTE FRANCISCO HERMANEZ TO PRESENT THE FOND PERSONAL GREETINGS OF THE PRESIDENT OF THE UNITED STATES AND THE SECRETARY OF STATE, AND TO INVITE HIS EXCELLENCY TO VISIT THE UNITED STATES AS THE PERSONAL GUEST OF THE AFOREMENTIONED WHENEVER HIS EXCELLENCY CAN FIND THE TIME.

3.   ALL EFFORTS WILL BE MADE, SHORT OF ASSASSINATION, TO SEPARATE HIS EXCELLENCY FROM COLONEL DE LA CHEVAUX. THE SECRETARY WOULD RATHER NOT HEAR THE DETAILS OF HOW YOU DO THIS. THE SECRETARY FEELS SURE THAT YOU ARE FULLY AWARE OF WHAT HAVOC COLONEL DE LA CHEVAUX HAS WROUGHT IN THE PAST UPON OFFICIAL U. S. GOVERNMENT FOREIGN POLICY, AND IS EQUALLY SURE THAT YOU KNOW WHAT WILL HAPPEN TO YOUR FUTURE DIPLOMATIC CAREER IF YOU BOTCH THIS.

SPARKMAN B. WATERHOUSE
CHIEF DEPUTY ASSISTANT UNDER-SECRETARY FOR PETROLEUM AFFAIRS

Somewhat later, a reply came:

FROM UNITED STATES EMBASSY, PARIS
TO THE DEPARTMENT OF STATE, WASHINGTON

1. WITH PROFOUND REGRET THE U.S. AMBASSADOR TO THE REPUBLIC OF FRANCE ADVISES THAT HE WAS UNABLE TO COMPLY WITH THE TELETYPE MESSAGE FROM THE DEPARTMENT OF STATE VIS A VIS HIS EXCELLENCY GENERAL EL PRESIDENTE FRANCISCO HERMANEZ AND COLONEL J. P. DE LA CHEVAUX.

2. THE FOLLOWING IS OFFERED IN EXTENUATION:

A. THE UNDERSIGNED PERSONALLY WENT TO ORLY FIELD AND WAS ON HAND WHEN THE CHEVAUX PETROLEUM CORPORATION 747 LANDED. SINCE THE SECRETARY HAS STATED THAT HE DOES NOT WISH TO KNOW THE DETAILS OF THE PLANNED OPERATION, I WILL NOT REPORT THAT THE UNDERSIGNED WAS ACCOMPANIED BY MEMBERS OF THE GENDARMERIE NATIONAL VICE SQUAD, WHO SOMEHOW HAD GOTTEN A TIP THAT THE AIRCRAFT CARRIED SIX TONS OF MARIJUANA PLACED ABOARD IT BY THE WELL-KNOWN AMERICAN GANGSTER CHEVAUX.

B. THESE FORCES WERE DENIED ACCESS TO THE AIRCRAFT BY OFFICIALS OF THE SURETÉ NATIONAL, ACTING AT THE REQUEST OF THE ROYAL HUSSIDIC EMBASSY. WHEN THE UNDERSIGNED POLITELY SUGGESTED TO THE FOREIGN MINISTER THAT THE LAW OF THE LAND SHOULD BE UPHELD AND COLONEL DE LA CHEVAUX PLACED IN THE BASTILLE, THE UNDERSIGNED WAS PLACED IN PROTECTIVE CUSTODY AND CONFINED TO THE VIP GENTLEMEN'S RESTROOM UNTIL THE AIRCRAFT HAD DEPARTED, MY DIPLOMATIC IMMUNITY NOTWITHSTANDING.

C. THE UNDERSIGNED LEARNED THROUGH A RELIABLE INFORMANT THAT HIS EXCELLENCY HAD COME TO PARIS TO VISIT HIS GRANDSON, ONE PANCHO HERMANEZ, DESCRIBED AS A HANDSOME YOUNG BALALAIKA PLAYER. THE UNDERSIGNED, TRYING JUST AS HARD AS HE KNOWS HOW, HAS ALSO LEARNED THAT THE GRANDSON HAS LEFT PARIS ABOARD A ROYAL HUSSIDIC AIR FORCE LE DISCORDE AIRCRAFT BOUND FOR SPRUCE HARBOR, MAINE. THE GRANDSON IS SUFFERING FROM AN UNDISCLOSED, BUT APPARENTLY QUITE SERIOUS, MEDICAL DISORDER, POSSIBLY OF A SOCIAL NATURE, WHICH HE ACQUIRED WHILE ASSOCIATING WITH BORIS ALEXANDROVICH KORSKY-RIMSAKOV.

D. ON BEING APPRISED OF THE SITUATION

OUTLINED ABOVE, HIS EXCELLENCY GENERAL EL PRESIDENTE FRANCISCO HERMANEZ IMMEDIATELY TOOK OFF AGAIN FOR THE UNITED STATES ABOARD THE 747 OF, AND IN THE COMPANY OF, COLONEL DE LA CHEVAUX.

    E. THE SAME USUALLY RELIABLE INFORMANT REPORTS THAT BOTH HIS EXCELLENCY AND CHEVAUX APPARENTLY HAVE BEEN DRINKING.

    3. THE UNDERSIGNED, WITH GREAT RELUCTANCE, ADVISES THE DEPARTMENT THAT THE WASHINGTON AMBASSADORS OF THE FRENCH REPUBLIC AND THE KINGDOM OF HUSSID ARE ABOUT TO REGISTER FORMAL COMPLAINTS VIS A VIS THE UNDERSIGNED. THEY QUITE UNJUSTIFIABLY CLAIM THAT THE UNDERSIGNED ATTEMPTED TO DISRUPT THE HARMONIOUS RELATIONSHIP WHICH EXISTS BETWEEN THOSE TWO GOVERNMENTS.

KENILWORTH T. JONES
U.S. AMBASSADOR

Air Hussid Eleven came in low over the ocean, lowered its landing gear, and touched down on Spruce Harbor International's runway number one, which also happened to be its only runway.

It taxied to the control tower and shut down its engines. The door opened, and the self-contained stair unfolded. Boris Alexandrovich Korsky-Rimsakov appeared in the doorway and raised his hand in greeting. "It is I, of course!" he said. "Boris Alexandrovich Korsky-Rimaskov. But no applause, please! I am here on an errand of mercy." And then he fell down the stairs.

Hawkeye Pierce ran to him, saw that he was unhurt, and raised his eyes to the doorway. Another gentleman was now in the doorway of the airplane. This one was dressed in a Homburg, a rolled umbrella, boxer shorts, and a "Harvard" T-shirt.

"I am very much afraid," Matthew Q. Framingham said, pronouncing each syllable with great care, "that old Boris is in his cups."

"Never mind me," Boris said somewhat thickly. "Attend, Hawkeye, in the name of Hippocrates, to the splendid young man aboard who gave his all for me."

"Where is he?" Hawkeye asked. "What's wrong with him?"

"Inside the airplane, brave beyond description on his bed of pain and agony," Boris said, struggling to his feet. "Rush to him, in the name of mercy!"

Hawkeye trotted up the stairs, pushed past Matthew Q. Framingham, and entered the small cabin of the airplane. All he saw that faintly resembled a bed of pain was one of the leather couches, on which sat a young man playing a balalaika.

Beside him sat Prince, on his haunches (which placed him about as high off the floor as the young man), his enormous tail wagging back and forth, a look of utter adoration in his eyes.

"Where's the patient?" Hawkeye asked. "For that matter, where's the bed of pain and agony?"

"It doesn't really hurt at all," the young man said.

"What doesn't really hurt at all?"

"What the doctor in Paris described as an inguinal hernia."

"You mean, all the noise Boris has been making is about an inguinal hernia? And how about knocking off with the music?"

"I'd really like to stop," the young man said. "I've been playing for hours. But whenever I stop, Prince starts to howl."

"That's strange," Hawkeye said. "I own his brother, and *he* only howls when I start to play my ukulele. But, to get to the bottom line, there's nothing wrong with you but an inguinal hernia?"

"I am sorry to have caused so much fuss," the young man said.

"I hope your fingers are strong," Hawkeye said. "You're going to have to play for another couple of hours. Six, I'd guess."

"Six more hours?"

"That's about what it'll take us to get to San Francisco," Hawkeye said. He went to the door and called to the others. "Everybody on board!" he said.

163

"Me, too, Doctor?" Barbara Ann Miller asked.

"You, too, sweetie," Hawkeye said, after a moment's barely perceptible hesitation. Trapper John and Dr Sattyn-Whiley, at the former's order, each grabbed one of Boris Alexandrovich Korsky-Rimsakov's arms and guided him back onto the plane. Hawkeye took Matthew Q. Framingham's arm and led him after them. Both of them were installed in seats at the very rear of the airplane.

The door closed, the engines restarted, and Air Hussid Eleven taxied to the end of the runway.

In the control tower, Wrong Way's radio said, "Spruce Harbor International, this is Air Force 1246. Request landing instructions."

"Air Force 1246, you are number one to land after Air Hussid Eleven, a Sabreliner on the active, takes off."

"Spruce Harbor," the pilot of the Air Force plane said, "in the name of the United States Government you are ordered to hold that Air Hussid aircraft on the ground!"

There came over the radio a series of grunting, wheezing, and snorting noises, followed by what sounded like two belches, and concluding with the words, "Air Hussid Eleven rolling." Clouds of unburned JP–4 fuel swirled out of the exhausts of the Sabreliner's engines; it began to roll, and in a matter of moments it was airborne.

"What was that?" the Air Force pilot asked.

"Federal regulations forbid me to repeat language like that on the radio," Wrong Way replied. "The bottom line is that he didn't want to wait."

"But I ordered you in the name of the U.S. Government to hold him on the ground."

"He probably saw that little old C–47 you're flying and figured you couldn't possibly be important," Wrong Way replied.

"Air Force 1246 over the outer marker and turning on final," the Air Force pilot said.

"Spruce Harbor International," still another voice

164

said. "Chevaux Petroleum One, a 747, requests landing instructions."

"Pilot of Chevaux One, this is Air Force 1246. Do not, repeat do not, atttempt to make a landing at Spruce Harbor."

"Why not?" Chevaux One asked.

"That you, Horsey?" Wrong Way asked.

"It's me, Wrong Way."

"You're number one to land, Horsey," Wrong Way said. "The winds are from the north at five; the altimeter is one niner niner. Watch out you don't run over the gooney-bird that just landed."

"Chevaux One turning on final," the radio said, and the enormous ship dropped out of the sky, touched down, reversed its engines, and skidded to a halt a good six feet from the Air Force gooney-bird.

The pilots of both aircraft descended from their respective cockpits, both making for the control tower.

The Air Force pilot accosted the Chevaux Petroleum pilot.

"Didn't you hear my message telling you not to try to land at Spruce Harbor International?"

"I asked you why," the pilot retorted.

"Because it is absolutely impossible to land a 747 at Spruce Harbor," the Air Force pilot snapped. "The runway's not only dirt, but it's only half as long as it has to be."

"Well," Horsey said, "you go tell the copilot that. He said I'd been drinking and insisted on landing himself." He turned now to Wrong Way. "Who was that that just left, Wrong Way?"

"Boris," Wrong Way replied. "He picked up Hawkeye and Trapper John and some other people."

"Damn," Horsey said. "Just missed them. Know where they were headed?"

"San Francisco," Wrong Way replied.

"Hey!" Horsey called three floors up to the copilot. "We got enough fuel to make 'Frisco?"

"Just barely," the copilot called down.

"Wind 'em up!" Horsey yelled.

Two minutes later, a radio message went out:

"Westover Air Force Base, this is Air Force 1246."

"Go ahead, 1246."

"Stand by to relay an operational immediate message to the Department of State."

"Standing by."

"To the Secretary of State from the chief deputy assistant under-secretary of state for petroleum affairs," the voice began. "The attempt to meet His Excellency General El Presidente Francisco Hermanez at Spruce Harbor, Maine, failed. His Excellency is presently en route to San Francisco, California, aboard Chevaux Petroleum 747 Number One. Please have replacement aircraft immediately dispatched to Spruce Harbor so that I can resume the pursuit."

In less than an hour—in other words, with remarkable rapidity for the Department of State—there was a reply.

"Inasmuch as the Air Force advises and the Federal Aviation Agency confirms that it is absolutely impossible for 747 aircraft to use Spruce Harbor International, it is presumed that that part of your message was garbled in transmission. Please furnish correct identification of aircraft in which His Excellency is traveling. Please also advise why it is necessary to send you a replacement aircraft. What happened to the C-47 you had?"

"Any reply, Mr. Chief Deputy Assistant Under-Secretary?" the Air Force pilot asked.

"*You* tell them that your lousy gooney-bird got blown over when the 747 took off," the chief deputy assistant under-secretary replied. "Despite my long years of faithful service, I somehow suspect they wouldn't believe me." And with that he leaned up against the upside-down fuselage of the gooney-bird and began to weep.

And at that moment, high over the northeastern United States, Matthew Q. Framingham, who had been resting up from the rigors of having walked all the way to the airplane's door back in Spruce Harbor,

166

suddenly woke up. He started for a moment in disbelief at what was going on up front in the cabin. And then he, too, began to cry.

The sound woke Boris Alexandrovich Korsky-Rimsakov, who had also been taking a little nap.

"What's with you?" he demanded, somewhat less than kindly. "You're disturbing my sleep, so it had really better be heart-breaking."

"It's heart-breaking all right," Matthew Q. Framingham sobbed. "Oh, cruel fate, oh, cold, cruel world!"

Boris, sensing that perhaps Matthew wanted to keep this just between them, whispered, "What the *hell* are you muttering about?" Boris whispered somewhat more loudly than normal people, though, and what he intended to be a discreet private inquiry took on more the character of a public-address announcement. Everyone in the plane turned to the sound of the voices.

"For a year," Matthew Q. Framingham said, "from the very first moment I saw her prancing around the bar of Sadie Shapiro's Strip Joint, I haven't been able to get her out of my mind."

"Shut up, Matthew!" Hawkeye said firmly.

"It's OK, Hawkeye," Boris said. "Matthew has got it bad for some stripteaser. One good look at her jugs, and he was swept off his feet."

"Both of you," Trapper John screamed, "shut up! Right now!"

"For a year," Matthew moaned on, "I have thought of nothing but her. I dreamed of the moment when I could return to San Francisco for another glimpse—"

"Matthew!" Hawkeye screamed.

"It's all *right,* Hawkeye," Barbara Ann Miller said.

"It is like hell," Trapper John said. "Shut up, Framingham, or I personally will turn you into the world's ugliest soprano!"

"For a week now, I have quite literally scoured the world for her," Matthew went on. "Dreaming of nothing but the moment when I could again see my beloved Betsy Boobs."

"Well," said Dr. Sattyn-Whiley, who wasn't entirely aware of what was going on, "I must say that's an appropriate name for a stripper. Had quite a pair, did she?"

"You shut up, too, Doc," Hawkeye said.

"And when I find her," Matthew concluded, tears running down his plump cheeks, "what is she doing? She's holding hands with another man, that's what she's doing!"

Since the only female aboard the aircraft holding hands with anyone was Barbara Ann Miller, Dr. Sattyn-Whiley was forced toward a certain conclusion, one that threw, so to speak, a new factor into his plans for the immediate future. What little doubt he was able to retain vanished when Matthew went on. "And on the wrist of the hand she's holding hands with is the watch I gave her! Oh, the perfidy of woman, not to mention the perfidy of fate!"

"I find this hard to believe, Barbara Ann," Dr. Cornelius E. Sattyn-Whiley said, "but I believe that drunk is speaking about you."

"My friend may have had a little nip or two," Boris said, "but let me tell you, Shorty, when he's talking about strippers, he knows what he's talking about."

"Thank you, Boris," Matthew said, modestly. "Betsy Boobs!" he cried. "How could you do this to me?"

"Am I correct in inferring that that drunk is known to you, Miss Miller?" Dr. Sattyn-Whiley said.

Barbara Ann Miller didn't reply. She stood up and fled into the cockpit.

Hawkeye and Trapper John sat with their hands over their faces.

Dr. Sattyn-Whiley got to his feet and marched down the aisle.

"Wait, I want to talk to you, Cornie," Hawkeye said.

"In just a moment," Dr. Sattyn-Whiley said.

"Now!" Trapper John said.

"In just a moment, Doctor," Dr. Sattyn-Whiley repeated, and kept on marching down the aisle.

"I would have a word with you, sir," he said to Matthew Q. Framingham.

"A fellow boob-fancier, are you?" Matthew Q. Framingham said, bravely fighting back his tears. "Hail fellow, well met! Sit down and have a libation with us. Misery, to coin a phrase, loves company. And I saw that she spurned your attentions, as, indeed, she spurned mine."

"Would you mind standing up, sir?" Dr. Sattyn-Whiley asked. When Mr. Framingham evidenced a little difficulty getting to his feet, Dr. Sattyn-Whiley helped him. Then he drew back his right fist and let him have a good one in the right eye. Mr. Framingham fell backward into Mr. Korsky-Rimsakov's lap, the force of his flight sending his skull back against Mr. Korsky-Rimsakov's head. There was a sound like that of a watermelon being dropped from the balcony into the orchestra pit, and then it was obvious that both Mr. Korsky-Rimsakov and Mr. Framingham were no longer among the conscious.

This fact, however, was not immediately apparent to Dr. Sattyn-Whiley. "If you ever again so much as whisper that lady's name aloud, fat mouth," he said, "I shall return and get the other eye and all your teeth!"

At that moment, the door to the cockpit was flung open. Barbara Ann Miller was standing there. It was obvious that she had been crying, but there was a look on her face that had nothing to do with sorrow.

"Hawkeye, you better listen to what's coming over the radio!"

"Put it on the speakers!" Hawkeye called. She turned to the pilot, and he threw the appropriate switch.

"This is Buffalo area control," the radio said, "with a warning to all aircraft in the area. A Learjet, marked Double-O Poppa, apparently flown by a madman, has just done a split-S and two barrel rolls over Niagara Falls. All aircraft are warned to stay out of his way."

"Dad!" Dr. Sattyn-Whiley said.

"St. Louis, here we come!" another voice said over the radio, removing any last doubts.

"Why would he want to go to St. Louis?" Dr. Sattyn-Whiley inquired.

Simultaneously, Hawkeye and Trapper John described an enormous arch with their hands and arms.

"Oh, no!" Dr. Sattyn-Whiley said. He put his hand to his forehead and said "Ouch!"

"What did you do to your hand?" Barbara Ann Miller asked.

"Nothing at all," Dr. Sattyn-Whiley protested through a wince.

"The first thing a surgeon must learn," Hawkeye said, "is that he must save his hands for the practice of his profession, and never, never use them as fists."

"In other words, Cornie," Trapper John said, "you should have hit old fat mouth with a champagne bottle."

"Let me see it," Barbara Ann Miller said, taking it in her own hands.

"I don't care what your course was," Hawkeye said to the pilot. "Head for St. Louis. Maybe we can talk some sense into him."

Over the radio came the strains of the "Fighter Pilot's Lament." The singer seemed to be anything but unhappy.

Chapter Thirteen

Dr. Frank Burns, after first installing Sweetie-Baby on the cable cars, rushed off to attend to his pressing business. He was so excited at the prospect of seeing his beloved Margaret again that he threw caution to the winds and flagged down a taxicab.

He found the First Missionary Church and Temple of the God Is Love in All Forms Christian Church, Inc., just where the Mark Hopkins bellboy had said he would find it, just off Market Street, under the sixth and final arrow shot from the Reverend Mother Margaret's bow.

He would have found it anyhow, he told himself, or it would have caught his eye, and he would have known what it was. It wasn't every day that you saw a thirty-foot statue of someone being welcomed into heaven, outlined in neon, and with provision for flood-lighting at night, sitting atop a six-story circular building painted lavender.

Getting into the building itself posed something of a problem. The streets surrounding the First Missionary Church were so crowded with people that half a dozen of San Francisco's finest, on horses, were having trouble maintaining order.*

---

* Although Frank Burns could not have known this, there were also two of San Francisco's finest, in civilian clothes, keeping a sharp eye on the building. If two Knob Hill swells like Colonel C. Edward Whiley and his son, Dr. Cornelius E. Sattyn-Whiley, were out on a three-day drunk, the odds were fifty-fifty that they would, for one reason or another, show up at the GILIAFCC, Inc., First Missionary Church and Temple.

"God bless you, my son," Frank Burns said, in lieu of a tip, as he left his taxicab.

"Screw you," the cabdriver, in the familiar jocular manner of San Francisco cabbies, replied. "You cheap son of a blap."

"Sticks and stones may break my bones," Frank Burns instantly replied, "but names will never hurt me."

And then, with the confidence of someone who knows where he is going and why, Frank Burns marched up the wide stairs to the main entrance. His eyes fell on a life-size cut-out of the Reverend Mother Emeritus, her arms widespread and holding a banner reading "Welcome, Sinner!" and he was so enthralled with what we will tactfully refer to as her muscle tone that he didn't see the large chap (he was, in fact, a tackle of the San Francisco Gladiators) guarding the door until he ran into him.

"And just where do you think you're going, little man?" the security person said. Frank Burns noticed that he sort of lisped.

"I'm here to see Hot Lips . . . I mean, the Reverend Mother."

"Have you an appointment?" the large lisping tackle asked, sort of pursing his lips.

"Actually, no," Frank Burns said. "But I'm sure that she'll be delighted to see me."

"Huh-mff," the tackle huh-mffed, rather nastily. "I would tell you you'd have to buy a ticket like everyone else, but the tickets are all gone."

"The Reverend Mother and I are old friends," Frank Burns protested. He then remembered his reversed, or clerical, collar. He pointed to it. "Would I lie about something like that?"

"Of course you would," the tackle lisped. "Now are you going to leave peacefully, or would you like me to help you?"

Frank Burns took out his wallet and produced his identification.

"I am Dr. Frank Burns, M.D.," he said. "A Fellow

172

of the American Tonsil, Adenoid and Vas Deferens Society. I *demand* to be admitted."

"I'll tell you what I'm going to do," the tackle said. "I'm going to let you speak with Brother De Wilde. Brother De Wilde is Reverend Mother's executive secretary, and he'll know whether you really are a friend, or are what I think you are."

He stepped out of the way, opened a door, and pointed down a corridor.

"Go down there," he said. "Knock on the door and ask for Brother De Wilde."

Frank did as he was told. After he knocked, a steel door opened to reveal another security person quite as large and ugly as the first, and smelling of the same Essence d'Amour.

"Well, little man?"

"Dr. Frank Burns, M.D., to see Brother De Wilde," Frank said firmly.

This security person took Frank by the arm and led him down another corridor to a closed door. On the door was lettered "REVEREND MOTHER EMERITUS. Knock and remove headgear before entering."

The security person knocked.

"Oh, God, *now* what?" a soft and pleasantly lilting voice replied. "What *is* that?" Frank could tell that the lady, whoever she was, was obviously overwrought.

"There's a Reverend Doctor out here to see the Reverend Mother," the security person replied. Frank noticed that he lisped even worse than the first one.

"Well, show him in, for God's sake!" the pleasantly lilting voice replied. Frank Burns put on his well-rehearsed face, the one he felt gave an aura much like the one Robert Young gave off on television —that of the wise and friendly but-don't-cross-me practitioner of the healing arts.

The door was opened for him and he marched in. He looked around for the secretary with the pleasantly lilting voice. All he saw was a small, balding male in tight trousers and a yellow shirt, who seemed to be totally surrounded by a cloud of My Sin.

"You're this Reverend Doctor person?" the little man said in a pleasantly lilting voice.

Frank nodded.

"Well," the little man said, "get to the point, dear. Jimmy de Wilde is busy, busy, busy. Are you one of ours, or did you choose this unfortunate moment in time and space to decide to come out of the closet?"

"I am Dr. Frank Burns, M.D.," Frank said. "I am an old friend of the Reverend Mother, and since I happened, by the wildest coincidence, to be in the neighborhood, I thought I would just drop in and say hello."

"No offense, sweetie," Jimmy de Wilde said, "but that's as lousy a story as I've heard in some time, and believe you me, I hear some corkers in here. Anyway, the Reverend Mother's not here yet. We're just about to go meet her plane. Nice try!"

"I know she's not here," Frank replied, desperate. "She telephoned me and said that I should come here and tell you to take me to meet her."

"That's a little better," Jimmy de Wilde replied. "Not good enough, of course, but better." He reached over to the desk, picked up a little silver bell, and rang it. In response to the delicate tinkle, the security person came back into the office.

"Throw this imposter out!" Jimmy de Wilde said. "But remember what I told you! No more broken arms!"

Frank Burns ran behind the coffee table. The security person advanced on him. Frank looked desperately around the room.

"Look there," he cried, with enormous relief. "There's my picture on the wall!"

"Just hold in that position a second, Bruce," Jimmy de Wilde said. "What picture?"

"That one!" Frank Burns said. "That's me."

"What's you?"

"The fellow wrapped in the plaster of Paris cast," Dr. Burns replied.

"I'll be damned," Jimmy de Wilde said. "It *is* you.

What happened to you, anyway, dear—get run over by a tank?"*

"You could put it that way," Dr. Burns said. "But that proves I'm what I am."

"I know what you are," Jimmy de Wilde said. "The question is whether or not you're lying."

"If I wasn't a very, very good friend of the Reverend Mother's," Frank said, "would she have my picture on the wall?"

"You may have a point," Jimmy de Wilde said. "I'll tell you what I'll do. I'll take you to the airport with us. If the Reverend Mother Emeritus is glad to see you, you're home free. If she's not, I'll give you to Bruce here, and this time I won't ruin his fun by telling him not to break your arms. What could be fairer than that?"

"Oh, Jimmy," Bruce said. "You have the wisdom of Solomon."

"Thank you, Bruce," Jimmy de Wilde said. "It's very nice of you to say so. Now put this person in the station wagon. I'll be out in just a minute. I have to have a last-minute chat with Police Commissioner Ohio."

When Jimmy de Wilde placed his call to Police Commissioner Boulder J. Ohio's unlisted number, the call was automatically relayed to the radio-telephone in the commissioner's official limousine, which he had just had returned to him from the Chinatown Precinct, and which was still full of rice and the distinctive aroma of something Commissioner Ohio didn't like to think about.

"Is that you, Commissioner?" M.** de Wilde inquired, very warmly. "Jimmy de Wilde here."

---

* The photograph on the Reverend Mother Emeritus' wall had been taken on the famous March 13 referred to previously, shortly after Dr. Burns had been discovered covered to his neck with plaster of Paris and with his arms wrapped around the 4077th MASH flagpole. The Reverend Mother Emeritus had kept it to remind herself of the tempting powers of Satan and the wages of sin.

** It was only fair, Jimmy de Wilde had some six months before decided, that if the ladies could insist on using the designation Ms., which left their arrangements something of a question, he, and others like him, should have the same privilege. Hence, he insisted on the prefix M., which was pronounced "Mmm."

"Hello, there, Mmm de Wilde," the commissioner replied. "I was just thinking about you."

"Oh, how nice! And I think about *you,* too. But business before pleasure, as I always say. We're about to leave for the airport. Is there anything you want to tell me?"

There was a good deal the commissioner wanted to tell Jimmy de Wilde. But he thought, *The little pansy's right again. Business before pleasure.*

"There are a few little things that have come up," the commissioner replied.

"Nothing, I hope, that will interfere with the Reverend Mother's agenda?"

"We'll try to let nothing interfere," the commissioner said. "But let me fill you in, just for your general information, Mmm de Wilde."

"Shoot, you great big hunk of man, you!" Jimmy de Wilde replied.

"Well, I've just heard that there will be some other VIPs at the airport," the commissioner said.

"You promised me we could have the whole airport to ourselves!" Jimmy de Wilde said. "You remember what happened last year, when that planeload of Alabama Baptists came back from Japan just as the Reverend Mother got here!"

"I have no control over this, Mmm de Wilde," the commissioner said. "There're two foreign dignitaries arriving, in separate planes, and some guy from the State Department who's coming to officially greet them."

"Who?"

"The son of the President of San Sebastian's due in first," Commissioner Ohio said. "Then the guy from the State Department, and finally the President of San Sebastian himself."

"Well, you could just send them off to some remote corner of the field, couldn't you?"

"We've already made arrangements to do that," the commissioner said, "so I don't really anticipate any problems. There is one more thing, however, I think I should tell you about."

"What's that?"

"There's a crazy pilot loose."

"I beg your pardon?"

"It just came in from the Federal Aviation Agency," Commissioner Ohio said. "Some guy in a stolen airplane. Started out on the East Coast. First he did a barrel roll in the gorge at Niagara Falls, and then he flew two loops around the arch in St. Louis."

"What do you mean, he flew loops around the St. Louis Arch?"

"Just what I said," the commissioner replied. "He flew under it, and then over the top. In circles, you see? He went around it twice."

"And what has that to do with us?"

"Nothing, I hope," the commissioner replied. "The last we heard, the Air Force had fighter planes chasing him around the Grand Canyon, trying to force him to land."

"And if they don't succeed, you think he's coming here?"

"I'd bet he's headed for Los Angeles," the commissioner said. "Theres a lot of fruits and nuts down there—no offense, Mmm de Wilde."

"Just watch it!" Jimmy de Wilde said. "You don't suppose there's any chance that he would come here and try to fly under the Golden Gate Bridge, do you?"

"Oh, I don't think so," the commissioner said.

"Why not?" Jimmy de Wilde pressed.

"Well, just between you and me, Mmm de Wilde, he may be crazy, but we don't think he's *crazy*, if you get my meaning."

"Frankly, no," Jimmy de Wilde said.

"Well, he has a radio, and they figure he must have heard about the Air Force's orders."

"What about them?"

"The Air Force has issued orders to shoot him down if he tries to fly under the Golden Gate. We figure he's not that crazy."

"I hope you're right," Jimmy de Wilde said. "Have you a time for the arrival of the Reverend Mother's plane?"

"It's due in in . . . let me see . . . in thirty minutes. I just got the word."

"Oh, my!" Jimmy de Wilde said. "I'll just have time to get there. Bye-bye, Commish!"

As the two Air Force F–101s raced through the Grand Canyon in hot, if futile, pursuit of Learjet Double-O Poppa, their maneuverings were watched from above by the passengers and crews of Air Hussid Eleven and Chevaux Petroleum One.

Radio communication had been established between the two aircraft shortly after both had taken off from Spruce Harbor, Maine. Because the Chevaux 747 was faster than the Air Hussid Sabreliner, it had assumed the role of chase plane, catching up with Colonel Whiley just as he made his first loop through the St. Louis Arch and circling above the arch while he made the second loop.

The Air Hussid aircraft had just appeared on the horizon when Colonel Whiley had set out for the Grand Canyon, and it hadn't caught up again until Colonel Whiley, a little bored with dodging the Air Force airplanes and with an eye on his "Fuel Remaining" gauge, had suddenly pulled out and headed for San Francisco.

"Air Defense Command, this is the commander, Fighter-Interceptor Flight Three."

"Go ahead, Fighter-Interceptor Three."

"Bandit has just left the Grand Canyon on a course of 270 degrees true. Estimated airspeed 560 knots, estimated altitude seventy-five feet. Efforts to order him to land have failed."

"Fighter-Interceptor Three, what do you mean, *failed?* Were you unable to establish communications with him?"

"Oh, we established communications with him all right. I pulled up right alongside him and signalled him to land."

"And?"

"He smiled and waved and then thumbed his nose at me, that's what he did. We are in pursuit."

"Fighter-Interceptor Three, if bandit aircraft maintains his present course, and looks as if he intends to fly under the Golden Gate Bridge, remember that your orders are to shoot him down."

"What for? He's not hurting anybody. As a matter of fact, he can really fly that Learjet. He's just out for a good time, that's all."

"It has been decided, Fighter-Interceptor Three, at the highest levels, that if it's a choice between the Golden Gate Bridge and one lousy private pilot, it's Sayonara, private pilot."

"Yes, sir," Fighter-Interceptor Three replied. "I'll shoot him down if he appears to be about to fly under the Golden Gate. And he's headed right for it."

"Hawkeye, did you hear that?" Horsey radioed.

"Just barely. Can you catch up to him before they shoot him down?"

"I'm on my way," Horsey replied.

"Fighter-Interceptor Three, Air Defense Command."

"Go ahead, Air Defense."

"Radar advises, believe it or not, that they have a blip of a 747 aircraft that is apparently descending from three zero thousand feet, estimated air speed 610 knots, on an interception course."

"Roger, Air Defense, I have him in sight."

"This is the Air Defense Command," the radio suddenly snapped. "All Air Force aircraft, stand by for an operational immediate message from headquarters, U.S. Air Force."

"Standing by," replied about two hundred pilots, all at once.

"Operational immediate message follows. From the Secretary of the Air Force, by direction of the President at the request of the Secretary of State. It has come to the attention of the President that General

El Presidente Francisco Hermanez, of the Republic of San Sebastian, is en route to San Francisco, California, aboard a 747 aircraft bearing markings, Chevaux Petroleum Corporation Number One. It has also been reliably reported that the pilot of the 747 has been drinking. All aircraft are to make all necessary efforts to locate the aircraft and to insure that it reaches its destination safely. End message. Acknowledge.'

About two hundred pilots, all at once, replied, "Roger, message received."

One pilot did not. He got on the radio this way:

"Air Defense Command, Fighter-Interceptor Three."

"Go ahead, Fighter-Interceptor Three."

"How about having it decided, at those highest levels you're talking about, whether you want me to shoot down the Learjet or insure that the Chevaux 747 reaches its destination safely."

"Fighter-Interceptor Three, what are you talking about?"

"Fighter-Interceptor Three advises Air Defense Command that a 747 aircraft bearing Chevaux Petroleum Corporation Number One markings has just leveled off at about one hundred feet, after diving from three zero thousand, and is directly above the Learjet with the crazy pilot aboard. I can't even see the Learjet, much less shoot it down."

"Stay where you are, Horsey!"

"Roger, Wilco, Hawkeye!"

"Air Defense Command, Fighter-Interceptor Three advises that both the Chevaux 747 and the Learjet are approximately ninety seconds from the Golden Gate Bridge. Please advise what action is to be taken."

"Fighter-Interceptor Three. Pray."

"Chevaux Petroleum One, Chevaux Petroleum Three."

"Go ahead, Mort," Horsey's voice said.

"We're about five minutes out of 'Frisco, Horsey. You need any help?"

"Thanks just the same, Mort. You go ahead and land. But tell Hot Lips not to leave the airport. She's either going to have to bury this guy or give him a good talking-to."

"Is he really going under the Golden Gate Bridge, Horsey?"

"Call me back in about fifteen seconds," Horsey replied, "and I'll let you know."

"California," Colonel Whiley's not entirely unpleasant singing voice came over the radio, "here I come, right back where I started from!"

"By God," said the now familiar voice of Fighter-Interceptor Three. "He did it! Nice flying, madman, whoever you are!"

Chapter Fourteen

San Francisco International, being a large airfield, has separate control facilities for aircraft in the air and aircraft on the ground. The ground-control operator seldom knows very much about what is happening in the air and cares less.

And so it came to pass that when Chevaux Petroleum Number Three touched down and the ground controller looked out his window and saw that it was a Chevaux Petroleum aircraft and a 747, he naturally presumed that it was the aircraft with the foreign dignitary aboard, and he got on his radio and ordered it to follow taxiway three to remote area "B," and there to shut down.

As he was doing this, a Learjet came in low over the field, did a barrel roll, made a 180-degree turn, came in, and landed without permission. Ground-control operator number one, who had his orders, was busy telling both airport security and the gentleman from the State Department that the airplane they had been worrying about was on the ground and on its way to remote area "B."

Ground-control operator number two was in command when the Learjet came in and did its victory barrel roll over the field. He came to the conclusion that not only was the pilot in gross violation of flight safety regulations, he was also more than likely the crazy pilot who had been disrupting the tranquil flow of air traffic across the nation.

"Crazy pilot of Learjet, you are ordered to taxi to remote area 'A', shut down, and await the arrival of law-enforcement officers. Boy, is your ass in a crack!"

He had barely finished saying this when he saw a 747 with Chevaux Petroleum markings touch down. He came to the natural conclusion that ground-control operator number one, who wasn't too reliable anyway, had missed the arrival of the airplane with the VIP dignitary aboard.

"Chevaux Petroleum aircraft, follow taxiway three to remote area 'B,' " he ordered.

"I heard you the first time," was the reply.

"Ah, Roger," somebody else said.

Police Commissioner Boulder J. Ohio, who had been monitoring the ground-control radio messages in his car, was making up his mind whether his duty lay with going to remote area "B" to supervise the security arrangements for the arriving VIP dignitary, or with going to remote area "A" to supervise the arrest of the maniac who had just done a barrel roll down the field, when his police radio sounded.

"Investigators three," the radio said, "for Commissioner Ohio."

"Go ahead," the commissioner replied.

"I thought we should report, Chief, that Dr. Grogarty just got here to the airfield."

"What's he doing out here?"

"Well, we told you that he's been getting all these messages from something called Air Hussid Eleven."

"No, you haven't told me anything of the kind," the commissioner replied.

"Harry, I thought you were supposed to have been telling the commissioner . . ." the radio said. Then, "Little slip-up, Commissioner. I thought Harry was doing it, and Harry thought I was doing it. You know how it is when you're conducting an around-the-clock surveillance. . . ."

"Get to the point, you idiot!"

"Well, all these messages say is that you-know-who is getting closer to San Francisco."

"No, I don't."

"No you don't what?"

"Know who you-know-who is," the commissioner replied.

"Neither do we, Chief," Harry confessed. "All we know is that when he got the last message—it said 'You-know-who is about thirty minutes out'—Dr. Grogarty got in an ambulance and rushed out here, sirens screaming."

"Where is he now?"

"We don't know, Chief," Harry said. "One of the traffic cops heard the siren and stopped traffic to let the ambulance through. We're stuck in a traffic jam."

"San Francisco ground control, Air Hussid Eleven requests taxi and parking instructions."

"Air Hussid Eleven, did we know you were coming?"

"Negative."

"You just can't land here uninvited and without reservations," ground control replied. "San Francisco International is a busy, busy airport. You should have known better."

"Sorry," Air Hussid said, "but we don't have enough fuel to go anyplace else. What should we do, sit here on the runway?"

"No, indeed," ground-control operator number two replied somewhat huffily. "You take taxiway three to remote area 'A' and shut down there. Just as soon as they finish arresting a crazy pilot, the airport police will get to you and issue a summons for landing without invitation."

Police Commissioner Boulder J. Ohio, his massive brow furrowed with thought, now made a decision. He would fix Dr. Aloysius J. Grogarty. He would arrest him instantly. If that didn't force him to divulge the whereabouts of Colonel C. Edward Whiley and Dr. Cornelius E. Sattyn-Whiley, he would take a drastic step. He would deliver the doctor to Mrs. Sattyn-Whiley. If anybody could make him 'fess up, she could.

"Attention," the commissioner said, somewhat sonorously, into his microphone. "All police in San Francisco International Airport, locate and apprehend Dr. Aloysius J. Grogarty, a white male Irishman with a prominent red nose. Notify me, the commissioner, personally, as soon as this is done. He was last seen in an ambulance."

He laid the microphone down. "Sweeney," he said. "Run over to remote area 'B' and we'll see that the arrival of the foreign dignitary goes smoothly. Thank God, we can be rid of him before the Reverend Mother gets here."

With a growl of its siren, the commissioner's official limousine raced toward remote area "B."

At just about that moment, patrol car Adam and Eve Six (manned by patrolman Sean O'Casey and Patrick F. O'Malley), which was on temporary duty at the airfield, saw a white Cadillac ambulance with THE GROGARTY CLINIC painted on its doors speeding down a taxiway.

"By God and begorra," patrolman O'Casey said to patrolman O'Malley, "there's a Grogarty Clinic ambulance. I'll bet me life O'Grogarty hisself is in it."

With a squeal of tires, its lights flashing and its whooper whooping, Adam and Eve Six set out in hot pursuit. In just a matter of moments, it had drawn up beside the ambulance and ordered it to a halt. Patrolmen O'Malley and O'Casey leaped from their car and rushed to the ambulance.

"And good day to ye, Aloysius," O'Malley said.

"I'm glad to see you, Sean," Dr. Grogarty said.

"I don't know how to tell ye this, Aloysius," O'Casey said. "It could very well be that he's been at the bottle again, but the thing is, Ohio, that lousy Englishman, has just issued an all-points bulletin for yer arrest. Now if ye'll jest get in the back of the car, we'll carry you back to the clinic, or wherever you want us to take you."

"I'm here to pick up a patient," Grogarty said. "I've got to get him to the hospital right away."

185

"Where is he?" O'Casey said. "We'll run interference for you, of course."

"I don't know. Could you find out where a just-landed Learjet is parked?"

"Consider it done," O'Malley said, and got on the radio. Moments later, with Adam and Eve Six leading and with siren screaming and lights flashing, the Grogarty Clinic ambulance headed for remote area "A."

Meanwhile, looking somewhat the worse for wear,* the chief deputy assistant under-secretary for petroleum affairs waited impatiently for the stairs to be placed against the side of a Chevaux Petroleum Corporation 747.

Finally they were, and the door opened.

The chief deputy assistant under-secretary for petroleum affairs saw an ornately costumed figure appear in the door of the stairs. He did not, actually, see this figure too clearly, for he had lost his contact lenses somewhere over Hobbs, New Mexico, and had been unable to find them in the cockpit of the F–111. However, this was a 747, and the individual at the door must be the ranking person aboard, because, following protocol, he had paused at the door and raised both arms in greeting. It was natural to presume that it was indeed General El Presidente Francisco Hermanez.

The chief deputy assistant under-secretary for petroleum affairs rushed up the stairway, bowed low, and made his little speech.

"Your Excellency," he said, "welcome to the United States. I bring the personal greetings of the President himself."

---

* In order to get him to San Francisco from Spruce Harbor in time to meet the airplane carrying General El Presidente Francisco Hermanez, it had been necessary for him to fly to Westover Air Force Base in a small aircraft and then to transfer to the fastest airplane in the Air Force inventory, an F-111 fighter bomber. The F-111 is a one-seat airplane, however, and although the pilot who had sat on his lap all the way from Westover to San Francisco was the smallest the Air Force had been able to find on short notice, it was still a long trip to make with a 168-pound pilot, in all his equipment, sitting on one's lap.

"Well, how sweet of you, and him too, of course," the Reverend Mother Emeritus said.

At that point, a man broke through the police lines. "Margaret!" he cried. "It is I, your Frank!"

He was immediately wrestled to the ground by two of San Francisco's finest, who, with eyes born of long experience with kooks and nuts, had been keeping a close watch on him.

The Reverend Mother didn't even see what was happening. She was, also from long experience, drawn to the sound of ambulance sirens. She looked across the grassy area separating remote area "A" from remote area "B" and saw the Grogarty ambulance, preceded by the police car, race up and skid to a stop beside a small jet airplane.

If she had not recognized Dr. Grogarty himself, she probably would not have done anything more about it, but she instantly realized that if Dr. Grogarty himself were attending to a patient, it must be a major medical catastrophe.

She turned to the nearest of the founding disciples —he was the football player who had remained behind in San Francisco with the writer to found the First Missionary Church, and as such he was accorded a place of honor in the arrival festivities.

"Butch," she said, "duty calls. I have to get over to that ambulance. Will you run interference for me?"

"You got it, Hot Lips . . . Reverend Mother," he said, and, raising his elbows to the defense position, trotted down the stairs and scattered those few spectators who had not fled at the sight of him from Hot Lips' path.

"It's me, Dr. Grogarty," Hot Lips shouted. "I'm coming!"

At that moment, the two policemen sitting on Dr. Frank Burns, M.D., rolled him over to get a good look at him.

"Now see here," Frank Burns said. "I'm Dr. Frank Burns, M.D."

"Like hell you are," the one policeman said. "I heard

187

what the lady just shouted. You're Dr. Grogarty, and we've been looking for you."

He pulled a walkie-talkie from his belt. "Commissioner Ohio, we got your Dr. Grogarty."

"Good work, men," Commissioner Ohio's voice came back immediately. "Tell him this is his last chance to tell me where Colonel Whiley is!"

"Where's Colonel Whiley?" the policeman dutifully inquired of Frank Burns.

"Where's who?"

"He won't talk, Commissioner!"

"Put him in handcuffs and deliver him to Mrs. C. Edward Sattyn-Whiley at the Sattyn-Whiley mansion," the commissioner replied.

"He's already handcuffed," the policeman replied.

"Well, then, chain him!" the commissioner replied.

As one of the policemen jerked Frank Burns to his feet, a representative of the San Francisco *Daily Bulletin* appeared.

"Hold him up so that I can get a good shot," he ordered. With one policeman beaming at the camera on each side of him, Frank Burns' photograph was taken.

As the Reverend Mother reached the Grogarty ambulance, Air Hussid Eleven taxied up and Hawkeye and Trapper John almost immediately burst out of it.

"Am I glad to see you!" Hawkeye said. "Unless it's too late."

Dr. Grogarty appeared at the door of the Learjet Double-O Poppa. He supported Colonel C. Edward Whiley, who was singing the final verses of "The Fighter Pilot's Lament" somewhat off-key, and with many slurred syllables.

"Drunk as an owl," Trapper John said. "We can't operate on him in that condition."

"I beg to differ, sir," Colonel Whiley said. "I haven't had a drink since that very nice little martini you were so good as to provide me with last night."

"He's been drinking something," Dr. Grogarty said.

"It's as plain as the nose on my face, which is to say, very plain indeed."

"I have not!" Colonel Whiley said, in righteous indignation. "Not a drop!"

"Get him in the ambulance anyway," Hawkeye said. "He's lucky he's alive, and I mean with his heart and lungs, not the drunken flying."

"Oxygen!" Trapper John said.

"Absolutely," Hawkeye said. "The minute you get him laid out in the ambulance, slap an oxygen mask on him."

"I mean he's already been on it," Trapper John said.

"What do you mean, already?"

"I mean he's been sucking on probably 100-percent oxygen from the moment he got in that plane. That would explain why he's still alive, and why he's obviously as drunk as an owl."

"I have," Colonel Whiley said, "been sniffing a *little* oxygen. As any old fighter pilot can tell you, it's the next best thing to booze."

Hawkeye went to Colonel Whiley and sniffed his breath.

"By God, you're right," he said. He propelled Colonel C. Edward Whiley toward the ambulance.

Mrs. C. Edward Sattyn-Whiley, who looked suspiciously as if she had been doing a little dignified crying, sat alone in the waiting room on the surgical floor of the Grogarty Clinic.

The door opened and three men entered the room. One of them wore an orange flying suit on the back of which was embroidered "Cajun Air Force." The second was attired in a somewhat mussed black suit. The third was dressed in a uniform of a type that Mrs. Sattyn-Whiley associated with what she considered the amusing but not very important works of Sigmund Romberg, such as *The Student Prince*. The uniformed gentleman was being held up by the other two.

"What are you doing in here?" Mrs. Sattyn-Whiley asked them.

"Same thing you are, lady," the man in the orange flight suit replied. "Waiting for good news from the operating room."

"That man there," Mrs. Sattyn-Whiley said to him, "is drunk."

"Madame," the man in the mussed suit said, "permit me to introduce myself. I am Sparkman B. Waterhouse, chief deputy assistant under-secretary for petroleum affairs."

"How do you do, Mr. Secretary?" Mrs. Sattyn-Whiley said.

"And let me state the official position of the United States Government, which it is your patriotic duty to follow, via à vis this gentleman."

"You mean that drunk in the comic-opera uniform?"

"Madame, you refer to His Excellency General Francisco Hermanez, El Presidente of San Sebastian. While it might reasonably be presumed from the way he smells that El Presidente has had a drink or two, I am sure that you will agree that it behooves us all to refrain from suggesting he's drunk."

"What's he doing in here?" she asked.

"I told you, the same thing you are," Horsey said. "Waiting for good news from the operating room. His grandson is in there."

"I see," she said. "My husband is in there. I have every hope, since I have secured the best possible medical care for him—"

"You didn't secure it—you got it, but you didn't get it," Horsey said.

"I beg your pardon?"

"Your husband's being cut by the two best surgeons around," Horsey said. "But you didn't get them for him. Aloysius Grogarty got them."

"How dare you!" she began, but then she collapsed. This time, the tears weren't discreet and lady-like. She cried like a frightened woman. Horsey's anger immediately vanished, and he tried to do the best thing he could do for her, but she refused his offer of his Old White Stagg Blended Kentucky Bourbon.

The door opened. Mrs. Sattyn-Whiley looked up

to see her son, in surgical greens, standing there beside a nurse similarly attired.

"You can relax, mother," Dr. Sattyn-Whiley said. "Dad'll be all right. We just came from the recovery room. He won't be flying any more for a while, but he'll be all right."

"Thank God!" Mrs. Sattyn-Whiley said. She turned to Horsey. "I think I will have a little sip now, if you don't mind." She turned up Horsey's flask and took several good pulls.

"And who, might I inquire, is this young woman?" she asked. She sounded like the Mrs. C. Edward Sattyn-Whiley of a few days before.

"Mother, this is Betsy Boobs," Dr. Sattyn-Whiley said. "Or at least that's the name she used when she was the headliner at Sadie Shapiro's Strip Joint."

"And what, Cornelius Dear, may I ask, are you telling me this for?"

"Because I'm going to marry her," Dr. Sattyn-Whiley said. "Just as soon as Dad can stand up with me. I thought you'd like to know."

Mrs. Sattyn-Whiley said nothing.

"We're ready for you, Doctor," a nurse said, putting her head in the door.

"Where are you going now?" Mrs. Sattyn-Whiley asked.

"I'm going to repair an inguinal hernia," he said. "On a friend of mine who's a balalaika player."

"My grandson," General El Presidente Francisco Hermanez said.

"Take it from me, Francisco," Horsey said. "If Hawkeye and Trapper John let this kid cut your grandson, he's all right."

"He is, after all," Mrs. Sattyn-Whiley said, *"my* son." She took another pull at Horsey's flask. "I suppose that if a chief of state can endure having a balalaika player for a grandson, I can learn to live with a terpsichorean ecdysiast for a daughter-in-law."

The door burst open again.

"Did I hear those glorious words, 'terpsichorean

191

ecdysiast'?" Matthew Q. Framingham inquired. "Where?"

"Will you, for the last time, knock it off, you stripper freak, you?" Boris Alexandrovich Korsky-Rimsakov said.

"My God!" Mrs. Sattyn-Whiley said. "I recognize you from your photographs. You're Boris Alexandrovich Korsky-Rimsakov!"

"How perceptive of you," Boris replied.

"The Grand Duke Boris Alexandrovich Korsky-Rimsakov!" She did a very nice curtsey. "Your Highness!"

"Do me a favor, lady," Boris Alexandrovich Korsky-Rimsakov said. "Hand me Horsey's flask before you fall down doing that and break it."